W9-CDY-238

Charm!

Charm!

a novel

by Kendall Hart

HYPERION
NEW YORK

ISBN: 978-1-4013-0307-5

Hyperion books are available for special promotions and premiums. For details contact Michael Rentas, Proprietary Markets, Hyperion, 77 West 66th Street, 12th floor, New York, New York 10023, or call 212-456-0133.

Design by Pauline Nenwirth

FIRST EDITION

10   9   8   7   6   5   4   3   2   1

Charm!

It was one of those brutally hot, muggy days in August when anyone with any sense was at the beach or by a mountain lake. But Avery Wilkins had many miles to go before she swam, and so she rode the subway to Finn Adams's office filled with determination.

Finn Adams was legendary—an adventure-loving, self-made business-man with the energy of six mortals, a visionary who had started a dozen companies, and whose door was always open for hungry young entrepreneurs.

Walking from the train to his office, down the stifling streets, Avery caught a glimpse of her reflection in a store window. The humidity had turned her auburn hair into a frizz-fest, and why was she wearing that light jacket over her sundress? She took it off, but felt too exposed. She put it back on. Oh God, could she really pull this off? A girl like her, with just a high school education, no business training, from a crummy little town, from a family like hers? Avery silently repeated the mantra that she turned to when she needed courage: "Be strong, dig deep, don't look back." She felt strength flow through her, infusing her with confidence.

Finn Adams didn't give a damn about the petty perks of power, and he bounded out from his office to greet Avery in the reception area. He was a tall, sinewy man in his late forties with a thick shock of black hair graying at the temples and a handsome weathered face. He wore a frayed denim shirt and scuffed-up khakis.

It was instant—pow!

The animal attraction, yes, but there was something more—they saw it in each other's face, that spark in the corner of their eyes, a recognition that they were kindred spirits, ravenous at the banquet of life.

As Finn led Avery into his office, he very gently touched the small of her back and sparks shot through her. He held out a chair for her, sat behind his desk, and said, "You have fifteen minutes to convince me you have what it takes."

It took Avery ten.

Finn wrote her a check for two million dollars in return for a 51 percent stake in Flair, her company. He also asked her out to dinner.

One dinner led to another and the fifth dinner led to a suite at the W Hotel.

The pent-up erotic energy between them was palpable, but as they rode up in the elevator what Avery felt most was trepidation.

She and Finn sat on the couch, and when he put his arm around her, she flinched.

"What's the matter?" he asked.

"Nothing."

"That's not true," Finn said, his cut-to-the-bone honesty softened by the kindness in his voice and eyes.

Something about that voice, those eyes, made Avery feel safe, protected. This was a man she could trust, who would never hurt her. And so she told him everything. The sad sordid truths that she had never revealed to anyone before. Her father had never hesitated to hit her when he wanted to make a point, and sometimes he did it just for fun, and she still equated a man's touch with emotional and physical pain. Then there was her mother, who had descended into a life of depravity after her father left. The combination of the two traumas had left Avery scarred—she was guarded and awkward in bed; sex had never been satisfying for her. Finn listened as the words poured out and when she was done Avery felt lighter, freer.

He held her, just held her, and slowly she relaxed in his arms. And slowly they made love, with Finn touching her so gently, so tenderly, until she was ready to touch him back . . . more than ready . . . hungry . . .

From that night on, for two blissful months, they couldn't get enough of each other. And it wasn't just the lovemaking. They simply adored being to-gether, and shared a voracious curiosity that took them on long walks to the farthest corners of the city, to lectures on art at the Metropolitan Museum, there was a hop up to Cape Cod on his plane. They would talk endlessly about everything, anything—or not talk at all.

Finn Adams and Avery Wilkins fell madly in love.

But there was a problem: Finn was married.

She was his second wife, a photographer who often traveled for her work. Finn respected and cared for her. The situation was hard, but he made it very clear to Avery that he wanted them to be together for the rest of their lives. They both agreed that their love should remain a secret until Finn had told his wife. He set the date. She was on assignment photographing tropical birds in the Caribbean; he was going to fly his plane down and tell her he wanted a divorce.

The night before he left, Avery and Finn went up to the observation deck at the Empire State Building. It was early November and a low fog hung over the city. They were above the fog, floating, so close to the stars Avery felt like she could reach up and touch them.

They kissed with their arms around each other, holding tight against the low fog below them and the cold, gorgeous ether above. After tomorrow, it would be like this forever. She pulled him closer to her . . .

It was the last time they touched.

IT WAS MONDAY morning. Avery was in the office, and she had a thousand and one things to do. That was why the sight of Parker—pretty petulant Parker—made her bristle.

"Hi, Avery, how's it going?" Parker said with that blazing bleached smile of hers. Then she sashayed into Avery's office like it was her own, plopped down onto the sofa, and crossed her legs.

"Things are hectic, of course. Aren't they always?"

Avery was the president of Flair, the cosmetics company she had founded four years earlier. She had started out mixing up small batches of mineral-based makeups in her tiny kitchen. Little by little, thanks to her talent, passion, and tenacity—and Finn Adams's money—the company had grown, but it was still miniscule by industry standards. Today, Flair was housed on one floor of a former warehouse building in Manhattan's far West Twenties and had almost fifty employees.

Avery was in the middle of developing her first perfume. She wanted the scent to be her signature product, one that would give

Flair a defining image and catapult it into the big leagues where it belonged. It would be the realization of her dreams, and the fulfillment of her promise to Finn.

"What are you working on?" Parker asked. As if she was really interested in the nuts and bolts of the company.

"Setting up consultations with perfumers, meetings with the ad agency, talking to buyers, arranging focus groups," Avery said.

"I want the perfume to have a sexy name and image," Parker said in that entitled private-school voice of hers.

That was so Parker—waltz in and make a sweeping pronouncement. She had no background in the cosmetics business, no idea what it took to run a company, to create a brand, to move a product from concept to reality. And she didn't grasp what Avery wanted to convey with the perfume. She wanted it to be romantic and sensual, not crass and overtly sexy. The marketplace was inundated with perfumes and beauty products that relied on a blatantly sexual image. Avery was determined to stand apart from the pack. And not to let Parker stand in her way.

But dealing with Parker was complicated for Avery; it triggered a swell of conflicting emotions. After all, she was Finn Adams's daughter. And she had inherited 51 percent of Flair two years earlier when her father died. It had taken them four days to find the floating debris of his plane in the Caribbean south of Puerto Rico. Finn's body was never recovered, claimed by the sea and its hungry creatures.

After he was officially declared dead, Parker—his only child, the product of his first marriage—came into the bulk of his fortune, including the controlling interest in Flair. When Parker turned her head a certain way or tapped her fingertips impatiently on the edge of a table, she seemed so much like her father, the first man Avery had ever fallen in love with . . . the man she loved still . . .

Sometimes Avery just wanted to tell Parker, "Your father and I were in love." But she and Finn had vowed to keep their love a secret until the day they could announce it to the world. The day that now would never come. But Avery felt it was important to stay true to their pact, to their secret. She carried it with her, a talisman, a touchstone that gave her strength and helped to keep Finn alive in her heart.

In so many ways, Parker was the opposite of her father. The pampered product of privilege, she had never worked a day in her life, and she treated Flair like her latest toy. If it failed, she could just shrug it off. For Avery, failure would mean the end of her lifelong dream. She wasn't going to let that happen. No way! She had worked too hard to get this far, to pull herself up from her bitter, twisted childhood in that shabby little house in Wilkes-Barre, Pennsylvania. She'd been paying her dues in the cosmetics business for over a decade. Unlike Parker, nobody had handed her anything.

"Avery, you seem tired today, are you all right?" Parker asked with insincere concern. She seemed very keyed up, and kept running her fingers through her long frosted hair and checking out her perfect nails. Parker had the best body money could buy—polished skin, toned limbs, gravity-defying breasts—and she clothed it in small clingy dresses twelve months a year.

"I'm fine, thanks," Avery answered, "just swamped."

"That's the problem with having big pretty eyes like you do— the circles really show," Parker said.

"Can we discuss the perfume another time?"

"No," Parker said. "I want the perfume to have a sexy image."

Avery stood up and walked around her desk. "Parker, I know sexy sells, but I also know that *romance* sells. Believe it or not, there are a lot of young women out there who long to love and be loved more than they yearn to be tacky sex goddesses. They're my market for the perfume."

Parker took all this in—and then tossed it out. "Well, I like sexy," she said with a determined pout.

"Guess what, Parker? I founded this company and it's my baby. You may own a big chunk of it, but you don't own me."

"Touchy-touchy. Oh, by the way, how's Marcus?"

"Marcus is fine, not that it's any of your business," Avery answered.

How dare Parker ask about Marcus Roland, the man she had been seeing for the past year? The man who had helped her finally accept that Finn was never coming back, the man she was getting serious about. The reason she was prying was obvious, of course. Parker wanted Marcus for herself. In fact, Avery had met Marcus at a party at Parker's downtown loft. Parker had been making a play for him, with no success. She was just jealous. After all, there are some things that even a bottomless bank account can't buy you.

"You certainly keep him on a tight leash. I haven't seen him at any of the clubs for ages," Parker said.

"If Marcus is on any length leash, he's there of his own free will. We're both adults. So keep your nose out of our relationship." Avery took a deep breath. She crossed to the display of Flair's products that she kept in her office. She looked down at the array of foundations, lipsticks, mascaras, powders. She picked up a powder compact. "Have you tried this new powder? It's been selling like crazy. It has a dusting of ground gold in it, for just a touch of sparkle. I think it would be fabulous on you."

Parker took the compact, opened it, and rubbed a little powder on the back of her hand. "Nice," she said. She snapped the compact shut and handed it back. "Too bad it's not my style."

"No, nice isn't your style, is it?" Avery said. "Listen, I have a conference call with a group of buyers out in Chicago. I need some time to prepare."

Parker shrugged. "Oh, that reminds me, I have an appointment with my personal buyer at Barneys." She crossed to the door and turned. "Ciao, darling, work hard." Then she was gone.

Avery closed her office door. She went over to the couch where Parker had been sitting, picked up the loose pillows, shook them out. Waltzing in and issuing edicts about the perfume was bad enough, but Parker's probing insinuations about Marcus were completely over the line. Avery was going to put a stop to them once and for all.

There was a knock on her door.

"Who is it?"

"It's me."

"Come in."

Justin Fowler walked in. Justin was Avery's right-hand everything. He pretty much ran Flair, leaving Avery free to concentrate on the products themselves and on shaping the company's image. Justin was pulling fifty, a battle-savvy veteran of the beauty biz. He was gay, a bit rotund, and wore round glasses that gave him an owlish appearance. Although he cultivated a jovial, charming persona, under it lay a tough, cunning customer who knew how to work every angle. Avery had seen him in action when she was working in the PR department at Clinique, and when she got her backing from Finn, he was the first person she called. He loved a challenge, but it was Avery's promise of 20 percent of profits that sealed the deal. Avery's instincts had been right—they hit it off immediately; he helped her navigate the intricacies of a cutthroat business, while she invigorated him with her passion and drive.

"You look all in, kiddo. Is everything all right?" Justin asked.

"Parker was just in here, making trouble as usual."

"Did she seem wired?"

"She was pretty keyed up," Avery said.

"My spies tell me she's been out at the clubs every night, partying hard."

"At least she's good at something."

"As you know, Parker has a history of serious drug binges that have led to some *very* bad behavior." Justin crossed to Avery's desk and said, "We have to treat her very gingerly, no matter how insufferable she gets."

"It's not easy."

"Remember, Avery, if Parker goes down, she can take the whole company with her."

"Over my dead body," Avery said.

2

IT WAS A gusty spring evening. High clouds skittered across the darkening sky as Avery and Marcus walked beside the ice skating rink in Rockefeller Center. This was one of Avery's favorite places in the city. She loved the elegant proportions of the art deco skyscrapers, the fountains, and the rink with its graceful skaters.

Avery and Marcus had seen very little of each other in the last few weeks. She had been working late most nights, or out of town visiting stores to try to convince them to stock Flair products. And Marcus's job as a producer on Timeline, a network newsmagazine, kept him working hours almost as long as hers.

"I feel like I haven't seen you in ages," Marcus said, putting an arm around her. He was such a hunk—a little over six feet tall, thirty years old, athletic, with ruddy cheeks from all the time he spent playing soccer and windsurfing, gorgeous green eyes, an unruly mop of thick auburn hair. Avery loved the glances that they garnered as a couple.

"I know, and I feel terrible about that," Avery said. "I think maybe I've got a slight case of OCD. No matter what I'm doing, half of me is always thinking about Flair."

"I must have a touch of it, too. No matter what I'm doing, half of me is thinking about you."

They kissed and Marcus moaned softly, pressing his body against hers.

"It's just that we have so much fun together," he said.

It was true—they did have fun together. Marcus had turned her into a devoted fan of the Brooklyn Cyclones, the Mets' minor-league team. Night games out at their Coney Island stadium were just about as good as it gets. He'd taken her on a balloon trip over the Hudson Valley and introduced her to abstract expressionist paintings. His energy and passion for life reminded her of Finn, although Marcus was a lot less mature. His privileged childhood in a fancy Chicago suburb had left him with a sense of entitlement, and he sometimes behaved like the rowdy frat boy he used to be.

"I promise to clear a whole day this weekend, just for us," Avery said. "We can take a drive up to the country."

"I'd rather spend the whole day in bed," Marcus said.

"That would work," she said, looking into his eyes.

"Listen, I know you have a business dinner tonight," Marcus said, "but why don't we hop a cab up to my place and grab an hour alone."

"I have to do a little more prep work for the dinner. I'm sorry, can you possibly blame it on my OCD?"

"Bad OCD!" he scolded, looking adorable.

They kissed again, he cupped her cheek, ran his hand down her neck. His touch sent a shiver through her body. She smelled his bracing mint soap.

When the kiss broke, she looked at her watch. "It's now a quarter to six. I have to be back at the office at six-thirty." She grabbed his hand and pulled him toward Fifth Avenue. "Come on, we have to find a cabbie willing to wait outside your building."

3

AVERY GULPED HER third cup of coffee and wolfed down a banana. She was always gulping and wolfing these days. She made a silent pledge to work toward becoming a sipper and a nibbler. She scanned her to-do list—it ran to three pages. There could be no doubt: it was going to be one of *those* days.

Justin knocked on her open office door and asked, "Are you ready for the cocktail party this evening?"

"Raring to go."

"Everyone who's anyone in the business is going to be there, including a lot of press and big out-of-town buyers."

"I brought along a little dress."

"Let's see."

"I thought you'd never ask."

Avery went to her office closet and took out a black dress with a narrow band of ruby silk on the hem and neckline. She held it up in front of her, looking at herself in the full-length mirror inside the closet door. At five-foot-nine, with lovely tapered legs, a long neck, and a beautiful angular face softened by her enormous eyes, she looked terrific in just about anything, but this dress was stunning.

"I found it in a little shop downtown," she said.

"It's perfect—elegant yet modern. You're a class act, kiddo," Justin said.

A class act. Avery loved hearing those words. In that dingy little house at 9 Mayflower Street in Wilkes-Barre, taste, tact, and black cocktail dresses were in short supply. Filth, misery, and intoxicants, however, were abundant. All during her childhood she had felt out of place, as if she didn't fit in with her own family, as if she really belonged in one of the nice, respectable families across town. She fantasized that one day a nice lady would arrive, tell her that a terrible mistake had been made, and take her to her new home. But the nice lady never came. So Avery would retreat to her room and fasten the hook-and-eye lock, and try to shut out the rage, sadness, and degeneracy that permeated the house like mold. Try to ignore what her father was doing to her mother, and later what her mother was doing to herself. She would lose herself in books, magazines, movies, studying the way girls like Julia Roberts and Uma Thurman spoke and moved and smiled, imagining life in a world filled with manners, culture, and wealth, and burning with determination to be a part of it. Now she was standing on the edge of that world, about to step into it.

"I've been in this business a long time," Justin said. "Avery Wilkins is a talented lady. We'll leave for the party at five-thirty." And then he was gone.

Justin would make the party fun. He would run interference, introduce her to key people, build buzz for Flair. There was so much riding on this perfume. Avery wanted to be famous, a brand—like Martha and Oprah, respected, trusted, loved. Maybe then she could finally stop running from her past, finally silence that voice that taunted her at 2 A.M.: "You think you're so much better than the rest of us, well, we're your family, Little Miss Perfect, like it or not. And you're no fucking better than we are!"

Just then Parker strolled into her office, looking like the cat that ate a dozen canaries.

"Hi, Parker, how are you?"

"I'm chillin', but how are *you*?" Parker said with exaggerated concern. Then she sat on the couch and tucked her legs up under her like she was settling in for a nice long girl talk. She took out a pack of cigarettes and lit up.

"No smoking in the office," Avery said.

Parker shot Avery a defiant look, took a puff, and said, "All work and no play makes Avery a dull girl."

Avery crossed to Parker, took the cigarette out of her hand, and ground it out on the inside of a wastebasket. "Was there something you wanted to discuss?"

"The perfume, of course."

"Go ahead."

"Hot!—with an exclamation point."

"Hot?"

"Yes, for the name. It's so simple, so sharp, so *right there*. Can't you see the ads: *Smell Hot!*"

Avery wanted to laugh, but she knew that Parker was serious. The thing about Parker was that underneath it all, she was desperately insecure. She knew she hadn't earned her position. Sometimes, when she came up with half-baked ideas like this one, there was a little flicker of doubt in her eyes, as if she knew her idea wasn't a good one, but that she'd just bully her way through. Avery didn't like bullies.

"*Hot* is all wrong for this perfume."

Parker shrugged, as if it hadn't been that important to begin with. "By the way, how's Marcus?" she asked.

"We agreed not to discuss Marcus," Avery said firmly, feeling her blood temperature rise a few degrees.

Parker ignored this. "I saw him last night at Play, he looked like he was having a very good time," she said.

Avery was caught off guard. She'd spoken to Marcus last night and he hadn't mentioned that he was going out to a club. And Play wasn't just any club—it was the club, attracted lots of boldface names, and had a reputation as party-and-pick-up central.

"I'm always happy to see Marcus enjoying himself," Avery managed.

"Oh, well in that case, you'll love these pictures I took last night," Parker said, pulling her cell phone out of her purse and crossing to Avery.

Before Avery could protest, Parker held up the phone and clicked through a series of photos. They showed an increasingly inebriated and uninhibited Marcus. There he was knocking back a shot of whiskey. Surrounded by three women, all of them laughing riotously. Knocking back another shot. Dancing wildly with a redhead in a halter top. Downing another shot. Tearing off his shirt to show off that soccer-taut torso. Making out with the redhead, both of their bodies glistening with sweat.

"I guess it hasn't been all work and no play for Marcus," Parker said.

Avery grabbed the cell phone and slammed it shut.

"I'm sorry, did I upset you?" Parker asked, wide-eyed.

"Parker, I know you want Marcus for yourself. Well, guess what? He's not interested in you."

"I've slept with him, you know."

"Once, a long time ago. I guess it wasn't very memorable. You just can't stand the fact that I make him happy."

"So happy that he's out picking up other women."

"Those could be old photos you downloaded."

"Now, that's what I call denial. I'm sorry, but if my boyfriend was cheating on me, I'd want to know it."

"That's what friends are for."

"You don't have to get sarcastic."

"Get out of my office," Avery said. She crossed to the door and stood there, looking Parker dead in the eye. Parker slowly walked out.

Avery slammed the door behind her, and sat down at her desk. The photos of Marcus drinking and kissing that redhead flashed in front of her. She'd trusted him. Now here was evidence that he wasn't what he seemed. That he had a side of him she didn't know about. And trusting men wasn't easy for Avery, not after her father, not after she'd given her heart to Finn Adams and then lost him so suddenly.

But what if those *were* old photographs? Marcus never denied his wild past. And Parker had known Marcus for years. Avery wouldn't put it past her to download some old photos. When you have nothing to do all day but shop and whine, it leaves a lot of time for making trouble.

Avery would get to the truth of the matter, deal with it directly. She picked up her phone and dialed Marcus's number. It was picked up on the third ring.

"Hello . . . ?" a woman's voice said.

"Don't answer that goddamn phone," she heard Marcus call out in the background.

Avery hung up and stood up, wanting to get away from the phone, from that voice. But she suddenly felt dizzy, as if she might faint, and she fell back into the chair with a strangled sob.

4

THERE'S NO PLACE in New York City more romantic than the Central Park Boathouse at dusk. It's nestled at the tip of a cove on the Lake's north shore, and its wall of windows looks out at the shimmering lake and across to Bethesda Terrace and the Angel of the Waters Fountain. The graceful angel holds a single iris in her hand, symbolizing hope and healing.

When Avery needed to think, recharge, or just walk off some steam, she would head over to the lake from her small Upper West Side apartment. It was the same apartment she'd lived in since she arrived in the city a decade earlier, not knowing a single soul, armed with nine hundred dollars, two suitcases, and a whole lot of moxie. For the first couple of years, she lived on tuna fish and peanut butter, and worked entry-level jobs in the cosmetics business. Central Park gave her a place to breathe, to take stock of the present and plan for the future. When she passed the Boathouse during those early years, she would look longingly at the well-dressed diners, eating, laughing, toasting. They seemed to live in a world brimming with pleasure and possibility, sparkly and glamorous.

And now here she was arriving at a fancy party at the same Boathouse. Before too long she would be releasing her perfume, arriving at her own party. And if the perfume sold as well as she hoped, she would move out of that little apartment, finally allow herself to enjoy the bounty of her labors. But for now she paid herself a relatively modest salary at Flair, and held on to her frugal ways, afraid that if she started to live large she would jinx her budding success.

She and Justin stepped out of the cab into the glittering crush of limousines and paparazzi. Inside the Boathouse, the scene was electric. There were beautiful people, beautiful clothes, flashing smiles, intense conversations, loud laughter. Avery spotted supermodels and industry titans.

"What's your pleasure?" Justin asked.

"How about a glass of wine . . . white."

"Well, I'm going to have a big fat double Mojito. When in Manhattan . . . Back in a flash," Justin said, heading over to the bar.

Avery stood there, the hubbub swirling around her, and wished Marcus were with her. *Yesterday's* Marcus, that is. Suddenly, in the midst of all the dazzle and buzz, she felt alone, vulnerable. His betrayal had shaken her. If her judgment about Marcus was wrong, what else could she be wrong about? Could she really make Flair a sustained winner and pull off the perfume? Was she out of her league? She heard that distant echo of her father's mocking voice. Was she a pretender, a fraud? Her throat felt dry and her pulse pounded in her temples.

Avery moved over to a window and looked out. The lake was luminous in the waning light, and there was the Angel of the Waters. She needed its strength.

"Beautiful," a man's voice said from behind her.

"Isn't it?" Avery said.

"I didn't mean the lake."

She turned. He wasn't tall, he wasn't dark, and he wasn't hand-some. Not classically at least, but it all worked—the slightly off-kilter smile, strong jaw, hazel eyes. He was compact, muscular, about forty, and there was something about the ironic twinkle in his eye that said, *This man is interesting.*

"You meant the statue," Avery said with her own ironic twinkle.

"I think she needs a new outfit. What are angels wearing these days?"

"Well, we know what the devil wears," Avery said. "Of course, she'll want to highlight those cheekbones with a little blush—from Flair, of course."

"Spoken like a true believer . . . Brad Henry."

"Avery Wilkins."

They shook hands, his grip was strong.

"I've heard that name. . . . Of course, you founded Flair."

"That's me. So you're in the business?"

"More or less. I'm in a lot of businesses. But mostly I'm at this party to ogle all the beautiful women."

He touched Avery's arm, lightly, not insistent, almost playful. A charge went through her. This man *was* interesting.

Justin appeared, looking very excited. "Here's your drink, kiddo."

Avery introduced the two men.

"Fantastic news—Suzee Jones wants to meet you," Justin said.

Suzee Jones was the editor-in-chief of *Stylish*, the wildly popular young women's magazine. Having your product featured in *Stylish* was like winning the lottery the same day you slept with George Clooney. The woman could make a career with a nod of her head.

"Let's go," Avery said.

"Well, we don't want to rush over like the fawning supplicants that we are, so let's just make our way there at a nice brisk pace. Brad, you'll excuse us?" Justin said.

"I know my place on this food chain," Brad said with a gracious smile. "Is it all right if I find you after your meeting with Suzee?"

Avery looked into his eyes and smiled.

Justin took her hand and led her through the throng. When they got about ten feet from Suzee Jones, Justin stopped.

"Not a good idea to stand next to her with our tongues hanging out," he said.

Suzee was in her mid-forties, tall and toned, with thick black hair and flawless white skin, wearing deep red lipstick that accentuated her full mouth. She was surrounded by a coterie of admirers.

A waiter appeared with a tray of hors d'oeuvres. Justin seized the opening and moved in.

"Suzee Jones, this is Avery Wilkins, the founder and president of Flair."

Suzee gave Avery a quick once-over and stuck out her hand. They shook.

"Nice to meet you. Your products are good," Suzee said.

"I'm developing a perfume I'm excited about," Avery said.

"I've heard that before," Suzee said.

"Never from me."

Suzee's eyes opened wide, and a little smile played at the corners of her mouth. "I'd like to hear more. Call me when it's ready."

Justin gently pulled Avery away. "You were brilliant, she adored you," he said as they melted back into the crowd.

"You think so?"

"Believe me, she doesn't ask everyone to call her. This could be *huge*."

As they moved through the room, Justin introduced Avery to editors, stylists, buyers. And then Brad was standing in front of them.

"I promise I haven't been stalking you," he said.

"That's disappointing," Avery said.

"Oh, all right, I have. How about dinner?"

"I'll leave you two. I've got asses to kiss before I sleep," Justin said before disappearing into the crowd.

"I really can't do dinner tonight, Brad, I'm just too beat. It's been a rough day."

"But everybody has to eat."

"That's why they invented microwave pizza." Avery's cell phone rang. She checked the incoming number, turned away from Brad, lowered her voice. "Hello, Marcus."

"That sounds frosty."

"Do you blame me?"

"No, but apparently you blame me," he said.

"As a matter of fact, I do. But this isn't a good time."

"It sounds like you're in Grand Central Station."

"Train's leaving," Avery said.

"You can be so cold sometimes."

"What's her name?"

"I forget."

"That's convenient."

"Come on, Avery, we need to talk. Give me ten minutes, name the time and place."

"How about never and nowhere?" Avery closed the phone and turned back to Brad. "I really have to get home."

"May I walk you out?"

The night air, fragrant with spring, felt delicious on Avery's skin.

"Why don't we walk over to Fifth Avenue, I'll hail you a cab there," Brad said.

They headed east. Central Park looked lovely in the deepening twilight. The street lamps were on, casting their mellow glow onto the rustling trees, a horse-drawn carriage clattered by.

"I love this town," Avery said.

"And apparently this town loves you."

They reached the Model Boat Pond, where children played with their tiny sailboats during the daytime, beside a statue of Hans Christian Andersen.

"I've seen pictures of Central Park from a hundred years ago, and this pond looked exactly the same," Avery said.

"I used to come here when I was kid," Brad said.

"Oh, you grew up in Manhattan?"

"Pretty much right across the street," he said, gesturing in the direction of Fifth Avenue.

"I'll try not to hold it against you," Avery said.

"Blame it on my parents."

They walked in silence for a moment and then Brad asked, "May I call you?"

"I'd like that."

Avery leaned into him, just a little. He put an arm around her waist. She made no move to pull away.

"I have a very strong desire to kiss you right now."

They stopped.

"You should know that I'm seeing someone," Avery said.

"So am I. I won't tell if you don't," Brad said.

"It's a deal."

His lips were rough, his body was strong, and grew stronger. Avery felt warmth spread through her body. It was a long kiss. When it ended, she rested her head on his chest and closed her eyes.

"Wow," he whispered, stroking her hair.

They walked over to Fifth Avenue in silence. As he stepped off the curb to hail a cab, Avery called in to her office voice mail. There was one message.

"Avery, this is your mother," the cultured voice said. "I know that sounds very odd, but I'll explain everything when I see you. I'm going to be in New York this week, and I'll be in touch."

A cab pulled up and Brad opened the door for her.

"Are you all right, Avery?"

". . . Yes . . . I'm fine . . ."

Avery got into the cab and sat there, stock still, as it pulled out into traffic.

Her mother suffered from alcohol-related Alzheimer's disease, lived in a group home in Wilkes-Barre, and was incapable of using a telephone.

5

AVERY WISHED SHE was one of those people who got up at 6 A.M., did an hour of exercise, ate a healthy breakfast, and then bounded off to work. Most days it didn't work out that way. Today was a most day. She overslept and woke up feeling distracted. And because she'd slept on one side all night, she was eligible for the Bad Hair Day Hall of Fame. Then there was last night's unnerving phone call from some woman claiming to be her mother. Even budding success sure brings out the crazies. Avery made a pot of coffee, and as it brewed she tried to pull herself into focus. Unfortunately, her focus kept going to Brad and that kiss, which wasn't where it needed to be. You don't get to the top of the heap by going all moony-eyed over some guy you spent twenty minutes with. The sooner she got to the office the better.

Avery dashed down the front steps of her building—and there was Marcus. He was wearing a gray suit, a white shirt, a blue silk tie. Damn him, did he have to be so handsome?

"Good morning, Avery," he said, sincere and serious.

"Hi, Marcus." She began to walk down the street.

"Can't we talk for five minutes?" he said, keeping pace.

"We're talking."

"I'm sorry about what happened. I'm under so much pressure at work. I needed to cut loose, have some fun."

"There are other ways to have fun than getting drunk and having a one-night stand. We're in a relationship and that's supposed to mean something. If you can't keep it in your pants, what's the point?"

"The point is we're good together."

"I'm sorry, Marcus, but there has to be trust."

"I don't deny it. I went out, got loaded, picked up a woman, and we had sex. Guilty as charged."

They reached the corner of Broadway and she started across.

"That's a big deal for me, Marcus."

"I realize that."

"And if you did it this early in our relationship, what does the future look like?"

"Things will be hard for a while," he said. "I know I'll have to earn your trust back."

"And don't you think part of the reason you did it was because you were angry with me?"

"I hadn't thought of that but, yeah, well, probably. You've been so damn busy. It's like, *If she's so into me, what gives?*"

Avery turned on him. "What gives? My future gives, that's what gives. This is make-or-break time for Flair, you know that. Couldn't you just bear with me for a little while? You bastard!"

Marcus stopped in his tracks. Avery picked up her pace, heading up the block toward the subway station. Marcus raced to catch up.

"All right, all right. You win. I'm a bastard. But I care about you, Avery, deeply, and I'm not letting go! You're going to have to fight to get rid of me." They reached the station and Avery started down the steps. "Because I love you!" Marcus called down after her.

Avery stopped. She turned. She looked up at him. . . . He meant it. He'd never said it before and he meant it. She felt elated, sad, confused, torn all at once. Part of her wanted to race up the steps and fall into his arms.

Then she remembered the pictures. Words were free. Doing the right thing took discipline and maturity.

Marcus's face was expectant, vulnerable.

"I'm sorry, Marcus, but those are just words."

And then she turned and dashed down the stairs.

6

IT WAS THURSDAY afternoon. Avery and Justin were in her office going over some sales figures. To their relief, Parker was out in L.A. doing what she did best—partying. She had a house in the Hollywood Hills and ran around with a wild crowd of rich kids and celebrities. Flair always operated much more smoothly when she wasn't around.

A deliveryman carrying a huge bouquet knocked on the open door.

"Please put them on the sideboard," Avery said.

The flowers were colorful and exotic. Avery crossed to them.

"Not bad. What does the card say?" Justin asked.

"They were out of forget-me-nots," she read, "but please don't forget me—Brad."

"That's his third bouquet in three days. I think the man likes you."

Avery couldn't resist a satisfied smile. Flowers from a man felt *sooo* good.

"By the way, Brad Henry is from an old New York family," Justin said. "There is some serious money there. They've endowed libraries, museum galleries. It's that kind of family."

"Interesting," Avery said with a little smile, half to herself. Then she turned her focus back to work. "Have we set anything up with a perfumer? We've got to get the scent nailed down."

"Yes, for the week after next. He's one of the best. His lab is over in New Jersey."

Genevieve, Avery's assistant, came on the intercom: "Parker Adams on line one."

"Should I take it?" Avery asked Justin.

"If you don't, she'll just call back every five minutes until you do."

"Put her through, Gen. . . . I'll put her on speaker. . . . Hi, Parker."

"Avery, I have incredible news!" Parker's voice filled the room—she sounded very up, too up.

"Great."

"I thought of the best name for the perfume!" There was a pause and then a snorting sound and then she started talking very fast. "So anyway I saw Paris Hilton last night and she loves me and I love her, it's intense our connection, it's like we're both rich girls and everyone thinks that just because you're rich and young and hot you have to be happy all the time, but I can't explain it, you aren't. Some days you wake up and it's all sunny and you just start crying." Parker choked up. "I'm sorry, Avery . . . Orgasm!"

Avery and Justin looked at each other: this was not good.

"Parker, are you all right?" Avery asked.

"I'm fabulous. That's the name for the perfume: Orgasm. It's fucking brilliant. Me and Paris were in the VIP lounge at Voom and it just like came to us both at the same time . . . it was a simultaneous orgasm!" And then she laughed hysterically.

"Okay, Parker, we'll consider that name," Avery said calmly.

"We're a brilliant team, Avery. See you next week, love you."

Avery and Justin just sat there stunned for a moment.

"Well, that was a fast-motion train wreck," Avery said.

"If she doesn't clean up her act, the whole company will get a bad rep. She's a loose cannon, and she's out every night."

"Let's keep her out in L.A. as much as possible," Avery said. "I'm not going to let her become a distraction."

"I just had a fabulous idea," Justin said, eyes twinkling.

"Yes?"

"Paris . . . and I don't mean Paris Hilton. I think we should take a trip there, just you and me. I know the city well, and it's the world center of perfume. There are perfume shops that date back to the nineteenth century. We can do research. Wait!" Justin stood up in excitement. "There's a master perfumer there, Henri Bihary, I worked with him once before. He's just amazing, one of the best in the world. I'm going to call him and see if he can possibly fit us in."

"That would be unbelievable," Avery said. "But can I afford the time away?"

"You can't *not* afford the time away. You're deep in the trenches right now and you need to come up for air, to see the world afresh. It will be good for you, and you've earned it. You've been through a lot," he said, brushing her hair back from her face, giving her a meaningful look.

Avery felt a swell of gratitude toward Justin. But there was something about his sentiment that she found threatening. She hated her vulnerability. She was afraid that if she ever faced the full truth of her childhood and her family, the sadness would overwhelm her. Keep that door shut tight. Her life was moving forward, what possible reason could there be for looking back?

After Justin was gone, Avery let herself savor the prospect of the trip. She wouldn't be going to Paris as a tourist, but to research her perfume. She was just starting to check out some Paris hotels on the web when there was a knock on her door.

Genevieve, who was in her early sixties and a total pro, poked her head in. "You're not going to believe who just walked into the office—Patricia Lucas."

"Patricia Lucas? Who used to be in the movies?"

"Bingo."

Patricia Lucas had been a respected actress in the early eighties. She had appeared in interesting films and was nominated for a best supporting Oscar. Like so many aging actresses, she had pretty much disappeared from sight, although she occasionally turned up as a guest star on television dramas. She was blond and delicate, and Avery had always found her winsome vulnerability appealing.

"Well, she wants to see you," Genevieve said.

"Did she say why?"

"No. I thought maybe you knew her."

Genevieve left, and moments later Patricia Lucas appeared in the doorway. She looked lovely, if a bit wan, in a beige linen pantsuit and white oxford shirt.

"May I come in?" she asked in a soft voice.

"Please," Avery said, standing.

The two women shook hands and sat.

"This is a pleasure, I'm such a fan of yours," Avery said.

"I can't tell you how much it means for me to hear that."

Avery waited for Patricia to say something more, but she just looked at Avery, studied her for a moment. Then her eyes filled with tears.

"I'm sorry, but I've been waiting a long time for this," she said with a quivery smile.

"I'm afraid I don't understand."

Patricia wiped a tear off her cheek and took a moment to compose herself. Then she took a deep breath, leaned forward, and said, "Avery, I know this is going to come as a terrible shock, and will take some explaining on my part, and some forgiveness on yours . . . but I'm your mother."

7

AVERY FROZE.

Patricia Lucas reached across the desk and put her hand over Avery's. "Don't have a heart attack, dear child."

Avery pulled her hand away.

"Is this a joke?" she asked, regaining some of her equilibrium.

"No, it's not a joke at all," Patricia said, looking into Avery's eyes with that mix of innocence and intensity that was her trademark.

Avery looked over at the classy, composed woman across her desk. Then an image of Jackie Wilkins, the woman who had raised her, flashed in her mind's eye: her puffy face, her cheap makeup, her sour smell, that dingy pink bathrobe she wore for days on end. In spite of the seedy picture, Avery felt a sudden intense loyalty to Jackie. She was her mother. How dare this woman just walk into her office out of the blue and make this wild claim?

Avery stood up, went to the window, and looked out. The sky was low, gray, and flat. She turned on Patricia Lucas. "I don't believe you."

Patricia was looking at her with a calm smile. "I think it's perfectly understandable that you feel that way."

Avery realized that Patricia had green eyes lightly flecked with amber, just like her own. Big deal. Lots of people have green eyes.

"Why did you come here? Why are you telling me this? Why now?" Avery asked.

"I'm hoping we can . . . get to know each other," Patricia said. "If you're not willing to take that step, I'll understand, but I felt I had to try."

"But you're not my mother. I've never heard of you, I was never told I was adopted."

"I'm sorry you weren't told."

"Will you please stop being so damn understanding about everything!"

"I know this is a lot for you to take in. Why don't I call you in a few days and see if you'd be willing to talk?" Patricia said. She stood up. "If you want me to take a DNA test, I certainly will. I'm your mother, Avery. I gave birth to you. I can't tell you how many times over the years I've thought about you, hoped you were doing well. My decision to give you up for adoption wasn't easy for me." Her eyes welled with tears again. "I'm so proud of you. Look at you, my precious baby girl. I just hope that someday you'll be able to forgive me."

"This is just so sudden, so shocking. I need some time."

"Take all the time you want. I've taken an apartment here in New York. I'm hoping to land some theater work. At my age, that's pretty much all that's available." Patricia let out a rueful laugh. "I'm so glad you didn't grow up to be an actress."

There was a tense pause. Then Patricia rushed across the office and threw her arms around Avery, hugged her tight.

"Oh, my baby, my baby girl . . . I've been wanting to do this since the second I walked into this room, to hold you, touch you . . . you feel so good . . . my precious baby girl . . . ," Patricia said, her tears flowing freely now.

This display was too much for Avery; it didn't feel real. She dropped her arms.

Patricia stepped back. "I'm sorry, please forgive me . . . ," she indicated her tears, "for this . . . and for everything."

Avery cleared her throat, moved back to her desk. "I've got an awful lot of work to do."

Patricia took a tissue out of her purse and blew her nose, dabbed at her eyes. "Is there any chance we can continue this conversation another time?"

Avery couldn't deny her intense curiosity. What if Patricia Lucas really was her mother? She took a deep breath and nodded.

"Maybe this weekend?" Patricia said. Avery didn't answer. "Have you been to the Cloisters?"

"Not for years," Avery said.

"It's my favorite place in New York. Why don't we meet there for lunch on Saturday?" Patricia said. "I'll explain everything."

8

AVERY COULDN'T GET to sleep. She was usually out cold by eleven, but here it was past two A.M. and she was still tossing and turning, reeling from her encounter with Patricia Lucas. The image of her saying *I'm your mother* ran through Avery's head again and again. Could it be true? And if Patricia Lucas *was* her mother, what did that mean? Avery would have to rethink so many of her beliefs about herself. That she came from generations of poor, uneducated people. That she was the first person in the family to lift herself up and out. If she was the daughter of a famous actress like Patricia Lucas . . . well, it was almost as if she was a different person. She felt a light sweat break out on her skin.

Then she felt that strange sense of loyalty to Frank and Jackie Wilkins again. But why should she feel anything for Frank Wilkins? He was a miserable excuse for a man who took out his frustration at life on his wife and daughter. Then he abandoned them, moved to Brownsville, Texas, and remarried. Today he lived on disability checks in a trailer park. Avery wondered if he was still smacking women around.

But Jackie was different. Yes, she was deeply wounded, self-destructive, completely unprepared for motherhood. Yes, she descended into the depths of depravity after Frank disappeared: all that booze, all those pills, all those men, so many men, a different man almost every night, the sounds of the creaking sofa, the low moans, the slaps, the filthy words, the twenty-dollar bills that would appear in the morning. Avery tossed off her blanket, flushed with shame. She had never told anyone except Finn the truth of what went on at 9 Mayflower Street. She could barely admit it to herself.

But still, in spite of everything, Jackie *had* raised her. When Avery was very little, she'd gotten her dressed and fed for school, taken her to the playground, tried to help with her homework, made a sad stab at being a mom.

Lying there listening to the muffled sounds of the city, Avery remembered her mother's sudden weeping fits, outbursts that terrified her. Avery would try and console her, ask her what was wrong, but her mother would just sit there at the kitchen table, her body shaking, her face red and tearstained. So Avery would sit on the floor nearby, her back against the cabinets, her legs pulled up, her cheek resting on her knees. She would wait for the tears to end, wait for the words she longed to hear: "Get me a can of beer, would you, honey?" Even the drinking was better than the black abyss of sorrow and tears.

But then there was that day. That one day. Avery was nine. Her mother had broken her leg after a drunken fall down the front steps and had spent three days in the hospital, the longest time she'd been clean and sober in years. It was a bleak, gusty day in late November. Avery was waiting by the front window for her mom to come home. She'd spent the three days cleaning the house, airing it out, filling the freezer with chicken pot pies and the cupboards with cans of soup. The cab pulled up in front, and Avery raced outside to help her mom up the front walk and into the house on her crutches. When they got inside, her mom took one look around, turned to Avery, and said: "Get out, sweet baby, get the hell out of this crummy town. You're too good for all this, get out and never look back." Then she'd gone into the kitchen and gotten out her bottle of Jack Daniel's.

The memory filled Avery with a sadness that descended on her like a wet blanket, suffocating her. She sat up in bed and turned on the bedside light. She reached for her phone and her address book, and then dialed a number she hadn't called in years.

"Yeah?"

"Hi, Frank, it's Avery."

There was a pause. Listening to him breathe, Avery felt a mix of revulsion and a strange, detached curiosity.

"Well-well, lookey who's calling her old dad."

"How are you?"

"Like you care."

"I don't want to fight, I just want to talk. Is that possible?"

"Why the hell are you calling me anyway? Your mother finally kick the bucket, the old cow?" There was a pause and she could hear him sigh and then crack open a can of beer. "All righty, shoot," he said, and she realized he was enjoying the attention.

"I met a woman today . . . she says that she's my birth mother, that you and Mom adopted me."

"That's bullshit, that's a total crock."

Why was there no surprise in his voice, just this instant heated denial?

"Is it a total crock, or are you a total crock?" Avery asked.

There was a long pause and Avery heard him light a cigarette

"Why do you want to haul all this up now? What goddamn difference does it make?"

"If I was adopted, I think I have a right to know it."

"Well, who is this woman anyway? Probably just some tramp that got knocked up."

"Women give up their children for a lot of reasons."

There was a pause.

"So how the hell are you, anyway? You ever miss your old dad?"

"I was thinking about you and Mom."

He burst out laughing. "The hell you were. You're just calling because you want something from me. Well, all right, you *were* adopted. You happy now?"

"I'm happy to know the truth."

"Do me a big favor, will ya?"

"What's that?"

"Leave me alone."

Then he hung up.

Avery threw off her covers and got out of bed. Sleep was out of the question. She *had* been adopted. Which meant that she wasn't the person she thought she was, the biological child of two embittered, uneducated, working-class losers. No wonder she had never felt like she belonged with them, no wonder there had always been that strange sense of detachment. Her mother was a famous actress, a woman of talent and poise and culture. Avery's identity had been reordered in the space of twelve hours. The thought was both terrifying and thrilling, a plunge into the unknown.

She walked into the bathroom and looked at herself in the mirror. She did have Patricia Lucas's beautiful green eyes. And her heart-shaped jaw. But what about inside? What aspects of Patricia's character did she possess? What was Patricia really like, under her careful façade? As she examined her face for clues to her new identity, Avery knew that something had shifted deep inside her.

9

CHEZ HENRI WAS the hottest new restaurant in the meatpacking district, a neighborhood of old brick slaughterhouses in the far West Village that had in the last few years become Manhattan's trendiest shopping and dining destination. Avery and Brad were having a late supper.

"So, tell me more about your childhood," Brad said, as they dug into their salads.

It was the question Avery always dreaded. She should have been prepared for it, but she never fully was. And now that she knew she had been adopted, it was even more complicated. She hesitated, took a piece of bread and pulled off a little bit. "Oh, my childhood was pretty uneventful. Middle-class, Wilkes-Barre, PA, usual milestones: ice skating, braces, boys." There were no ice skates, no braces, no boys.

"I bet you were adorable in braces," Brad said.

"You, on the other hand, are an American aristocrat," Avery said, eager to change the subject.

"And we all know what happens to aristocrats," Brad said.

"They marry other aristocrats, buy houses on Nantucket, and have beautiful children?"

Brad laughed. "Wrong. They live on gin and entitlement, and become sodden bores. You're right about the house on Nantucket, though."

"But that hasn't happened to you," Avery said.

"Nantucket bores the hell out of me and gin gives me a headache. God, you're an attractive woman," he said.

"Thank you."

"Why do I get the feeling, though, that you're holding something back?"

Avery felt a flush rise in her cheeks. People would judge her if they knew the truth; it would hurt her career, lessen her, cheapen her. Brad would drop her like a hot potato. Once again she opted for deflection. "Maybe you're projecting?" she said.

"Oh, you think I may be holding something back?"

"You never know," Avery said.

"Busted." Brad took a long sip of his wine. "I have two failed marriages behind me."

"That must have been very painful."

"The failure of the second marriage wasn't pretty. The first one, not so much. It was a starter marriage. We were both kids and I think we realized pretty quickly that we were all wrong for each other. She just wanted to live out in Sun Valley and ski and ride her horse. I need to work, and I love cities. We parted friends after two years."

"And the second?"

Brad's face darkened. "That was uglier. But let's not get into it. This dinner is about us."

There was a pause and the restaurant seemed to recede around them. Their table became an intimate space. It was just the two of them, a man and woman who realized that they clicked. The physical attraction was there, the easy banter was there . . . but this was the next step. They leaned into each other, dropped their voices.

"There is something I should tell you about my past," Avery said. "I . . ."

"Yes?"

"I . . . I was adopted."

"Well, that's hardly a deep dark secret."

"I know, it's just that a woman has appeared in my life claiming that she's my birth mother."

Avery told him about Patricia Lucas.

"What a fascinating story," he said. "How do you feel about it?"

"I feel a lot of things, all at once. Confused, excited, angry, relieved. It's been a roller coaster. What's really struck me is the loyalty I feel towards my adoptive parents."

"You should feel loyal to them, they were obviously wonderful parents."

Avery took a sip of her wine and wished the food would arrive.

A well-dressed man about Brad's age approached the table. "Brad Henry, how the hell are you?"

Brad looked taken aback for a second, but quickly recovered. "Hi, Josh, how are you? Josh Marshall, this is Avery Wilkins."

"Hi, Avery Wilkins," Josh said with a smile. Then he turned back to Brad. "So, when did you move back from Seattle?"

"About six months ago."

"I'm glad all that unpleasantness is behind you," Josh said.

"It was no fun," Brad said.

"Well, you've certainly been keeping a low profile since you got back," Josh said.

Brad took a sip of wine. "Been busy," he said, with a dismissive edge in his voice.

"Well, don't be a stranger. Nice to meet you, Avery." Then he turned and left.

"I didn't know you lived in Seattle," Avery said.

Brad buttered a piece of bread, and Avery felt like he was avoiding looking her in the eyes. "Yes, I lived out there for five years, that's where my second marriage imploded. And yes, it was unpleasant."

Something in his tone told Avery not to pursue the subject. "And Josh is an old friend?"

"We went to Princeton together. We started a poker game in the dorm and he still keeps it going. I used to join in when I was in town."

"But you haven't rejoined since you moved back?"

"Nah, I always lost," Brad said with a laugh. "I'm not very good at keeping a poker face."

"I'm not sure I believe that," Avery said.

10

SATURDAY WAS A glorious spring day. There wasn't a cloud in the sky, and the air was fresh and dry. Avery took the subway uptown to meet Patricia Lucas. The Cloisters was one of the city's great treasures, a museum of medieval art that sat on a rock outcropping near the northern tip of Manhattan. The graceful Gothic building was assembled from stones and arches and wooden panels imported from five French cloisters. Visiting the museum, with its vaulted arcades and calm cool courtyards, was like stepping back into the thirteenth century.

As she walked from the station to the museum, Avery was conflicted. She wanted to be open-minded, but how could Patricia just abandon her own daughter like that? While she was a famous and wealthy actress, Avery could barely afford to pay for her school lunch and wore thrift-shop clothes. And why did she suddenly decide she wanted to contact Avery now? What were her true motives?

Patricia was waiting on the front steps of the museum, and she waved to Avery as she approached. She was wearing cream slacks and a pale green silk blouse. She looked pretty but self-conscious, as if she couldn't quite relax.

"Good morning, Avery."

"Hi, Patricia."

The two women exchanged a quick kiss on the cheek. There was a formality and wariness between them, as if they were old friends who'd had a fight and were meeting to try to patch things up.

"I've always loved it up here," Patricia said as they made their way through the galleries. "This building stirs my soul. It's a testament to the power of art to put us in touch with our best selves." She gave Avery a meaningful look.

They found themselves in a gallery that held seven large tapestries that told the story of the hunt for a unicorn.

"Aren't they glorious?" Patricia said in a hushed voice. "Just imagine the weavers creating these over five hundred years ago. The unicorn was believed to have magical powers." She was captivated; her eyes were wide with wonder. But it was all a little overdone. Avery almost felt like there was a camera rolling.

"I'd rather talk than look at antiquities," Avery said.

"Of course."

They walked outside and sat on a bench overlooking the Hudson River, glistening in the bright sunshine. Just to the south was the George Washington Bridge and beyond that the towers of lower Manhattan. Directly across the river were the New Jersey Palisades, sheer cliffs that rose up from the riverbank.

"I'd forgotten how beautiful New York is," Patricia said.

"Have you ever lived here?"

"I haven't. I was born and raised in northern California and moved to Los Angeles when I was seventeen, the day after I graduated high school."

"I moved to New York when I was seventeen, the day after I graduated high school," Avery said.

"That's a pretty amazing coincidence," Patricia said. The two women looked at each other—a tenuous connection was made. "I hope you had a little more sense than I did at that age. I was such a headstrong girl."

"What was your family like?" Avery asked.

"I'm an only child. My parents—your grandparents—were very proper people. Dad ran an insurance agency, Mom was your typical homemaker. It was church every Sunday, dinner at six every night, strict curfew, pure white bread. When I got to Los Angeles, I felt like I'd been set free. I went a little overboard."

"You mean . . . ?"

"I wanted to bite into life, experience it. It was a wild time, the seventies. There was a sexual revolution going on. I signed up for duty."

"And you got pregnant?"

Patricia nodded and looked off into the distance, eyes unfocused. "I remember the day I found out. It was a brutally hot June afternoon. Of course I suspected I was pregnant when my period was late, but hearing those words: 'You're going to have a baby.' . . . When I think of all the women who long to hear that . . . and I felt like I'd been slapped, punished for my behavior. I walked out of the doctor's office in shock. I was just a kid, I had no money."

"Where was . . . my father?"

"Who knows? Long gone. Avery, it was a very different time. Girls and boys were just, well . . . in retrospect I'd say we were pretending there were no consequences to our actions. At the time we told ourselves we were breaking boundaries, being free, having fun."

"You're saying my father was a one-night stand?"

"Couldn't we just call it a very brief affair?"

This was another blow for Avery to absorb. She was the product of a meaningless fling, and she would never know who her father was.

Two middle-aged women approached, beaming. "We're sorry to interrupt, but we just had to tell you what fans we are," one of them said to Patricia.

"We just love you," the other added.

"Thank you so much." Patricia gave them a radiant smile. Avery was amazed at how Patricia could turn on her charm like it was a light switch. What would these women think if they knew of her wild past, of the daughter she had abandoned?

"And you're much more beautiful in person," the first woman said.

"You're very kind," Patricia said.

The two women just stood there, silently gushing. Then Avery felt something that surprised her—a surge of pride and reflected glory. Her mother was a gifted actress and a celebrity.

"Do you have any movies coming up?" the first woman asked.

Was that annoyance that flashed across Patricia's face? "Thank you for asking. I'm working on a few projects."

"What about television, anything on television?"

"I just moved east to talk to some directors who are trying to lure me onto the stage," Patricia said, a note of irritation in her voice. She clapped her hands together and said, "This is my daughter, Avery Wilkins. I think she's going to be more famous than I ever was."

The two women turned to Avery, eager smiles on their faces. Avery thought: so this is what it feels like to be famous, this instant unearned acceptance and goodwill. Everything Avery had, she had earned.

"Oh, really? Are you an actress?" one of the women asked excitedly.

"No, I have a cosmetics company, Flair."

"You're kidding? My daughter bought me a Flair lipstick just last week."

"Do you like it?" Avery asked.

"The color is so rich, and my daughter loves your products."

Avery was happy that Patricia was hearing this.

"Well, you two certainly are an illustrious mother-daughter duo. Our girlfriends aren't going to believe this," the other woman said. "But we'll leave you alone now."

The women left, both pulling out their cell phones as they went.

"Fans," Patricia said, almost to herself, "they can be very intrusive." Then she shook her head and her tone changed back to warm and bright. "Well, Avery, we're an illustrious mother-daughter duo."

Avery was a long way from thinking of Patricia as her mother. She was charming, and her celebrity status had undeniable appeal, but there was something about her that Avery just didn't trust.

"So, you found yourself pregnant?" she asked, wanting to hear the rest of the story.

"Yes, pregnant and alone. I was working as a waitress. I had very little money. Telling my parents was out of the question. I was scared. I was nowhere near ready to have a child. The truth is I was just a child myself. I wanted to experience life and pursue a career, not be tied to a baby. I suppose if I'd had more of a relationship with your father, I would have felt more emotional attachment to the life inside me. But the timing was so bad, I was so unprepared. You can understand that, can't you?"

"I'm trying," Avery said. "But it hurts to be referred to as a nuisance, an impediment, rather than as a person."

"I know, darling, and I'm sorry, but I want to be honest with you," Patricia said. "I seriously considered an abortion. My friends were encouraging me. It would have been convenient. I had just found an agent. I was very ambitious."

"What dissuaded you?"

"I wish I could say it was a reverence for life or something similarly high-minded, but I was just terrified of the operation itself. There were so many horror stories of botched abortions, deaths, permanent damage." Patricia reached out and squeezed Avery's hand. "I can't tell you how good it feels to finally be telling you this."

"It's not easy to hear it."

"One of my girlfriends was from back east, Pennsylvania. She told me that her aunt and uncle had helped other girls. She said I could stay with them and they would help me put the baby up for adoption. . . ." Patricia stopped and looked down at her hands, swallowed. "You know, this isn't easy for me, either. Reliving all of it. It was a painful time. I felt so guilty—for getting pregnant in the first place, for considering an abortion, for giving you up."

You should feel guilty, Avery thought.

"So I waited until I started to show and then I moved to Wilkes-Barre for three months."

"What was that like?"

"It was horrible. They were a very devout couple and could barely contain their disapproval. I had sinned and they wanted me to suffer. The atmosphere was oppressive. All I wanted was to get the birth over with and get back to Los Angeles and my career. Does that make me sound like a monster?"

"It makes you sound selfish."

"Well, I guess I was. But I had to be. I was alone."

"So you gave birth and then put me up for adoption?"

"Yes, it was a Catholic hospital. They took you away from me right away. I got to hold you once and then you were gone. . . ." Patricia looked down, and when she looked up her eyes were filled with tears.

Avery couldn't shake the feeling that she was watching a performance. And Patricia hadn't asked her a single question about her own childhood, about her adoptive parents, about her early years in New York.

"So then you went back to Los Angeles and concentrated on your career?"

Patricia took out a tissue and wiped at her eyes. "Yes, yes, I did. I threw myself into it, at least partly to escape my guilt." She took a pack of cigarettes out of her purse and lit one. She exhaled and said, "I don't smoke."

Avery looked out at the view, feeling numb. How could Patricia have given her up so easily, allowed her to be raised by such terrible people, waited until now to get in touch? Avery had never felt like she belonged with Frank and Jackie Wilkins, but she certainly didn't feel like she belonged with Patricia Lucas, either.

"I have some other news for you," Patricia said.

"Yes?"

"You have a sister."

Avery let out an involuntary gasp. "I do!?"

"Yes. Well, a half-sister. From my second marriage."

Just as Avery was beginning to wrap her mind around the fact that Patricia Lucas was her birth mother, she got this surprise. "Does she know about me?"

"I just told her. She lives in Brooklyn. Her name is Lucy, Lucy Charles."

Avery's shock gave way to intense curiosity. She had a sister. A baby sister.

"May I give her your phone number?"

Avery nodded.

The two women sat in silence for a little while.

"Are you feeling better . . . about us?" Patricia asked finally.

Avery hesitated a moment before saying, "I still have more questions than answers."

AVERY WAS AT her desk going over ad copy, when Justin strode into the office.

"Fantastic news!" he said exultantly.

"Yes?"

"I just got off the phone with Henri Bihary, the master perfumer in Paris. He'll see us!"

A tingle raced up Avery's spine. "You're a wizard! How did you do it?"

"A lot of sweet talk . . . and a big fat bonus."

"And he's good?"

"He's remarkable. This perfume is going to be amazing."

"And we're going to be in Paris," Avery said.

"Let me go firm up our travel arrangements," Justin said.

When he left, Avery tried to bring her focus back to the ad copy, but it wasn't easy, not with Paris beckoning. The trip was exactly what she needed to take her mind off Patricia Lucas. She had re-played their meeting at the Cloisters in her head over and over. And the more she thought about it, the angrier she got. The woman was clearly a manipulator. Why had she chosen to suddenly appear in Avery's life now? What did she want from her? And why? Those questions haunted Avery, and before she would let Patricia into her life—and maybe even into her heart—she was going to make damn sure she was satisfied with the answers.

Her phone rang.

"Hello."

"Is this Avery?" asked a young woman.

"Yes, who is this?"

"It's Lucy, Lucy Charles . . . your sister."

How strange those words sounded: *your sister.* Avery had already decided that she wasn't going to hold Patricia's behavior against Lucy. She wanted them to have a clean slate, and to build a relationship based on their blood bond. When she was a little girl, she had often yearned for a sister—to ride her bike down to the river with, to talk and laugh and fight with. An ally to help her fend off her dad and take care of her mom. Someone who would be supportive no matter what, who she could count on in times of trouble, and turn to for advice and comfort. And now she did.

"Lucy, hi," she said.

There was a funny silence.

"Does this feel as weird to you as it does to me?" Lucy asked.

"Probably weirder. But exciting."

The two women laughed. Avery could hardly believe she was having this conversation. "I don't know where to begin, except to say that I'd love to meet you. That is, if you're interested," Lucy said.

"Interested? Are you kidding me?" Avery said. "It's not every day you find out you have a sister. I'm dying to meet you."

"Oh God, me too. Mom said you were fabulous."

Avery was brought up short by the way Lucy said "Mom,"

meaning their mom. Patricia Lucas may have been her biological mother, but she was nowhere near accepting her as her "mom."

"That's nice to hear. Is there any chance you'd like to go out for a late supper tonight?" Avery asked.

"Name the time and place."

"Can you meet me at my office at eight?"

"See you then."

Avery hung up. Lucy sounded bright, enthusiastic, fun. She couldn't wait to see what she looked like, to get to know her. Avery was acutely aware that she had no real family. At holidays, her friends and colleagues would be rushing off to visit their families, hectically buying presents, making plans, anticipating rowdy, affectionate dinners and games of touch football. Avery had spent a lot of holidays sitting alone in a movie theater, waiting for the day to be over. Now everything was different.

Avery had a wild urge to get up and race around Flair's offices telling everyone: *Guess what, I've got a sister! A sister!* But she managed to contain herself. Still, she couldn't wait to meet Lucy, to become friends, more than friends . . . family.

12

THE SIX GOLDEN Lab puppies bounded over to Avery and swirled around her legs—rowdy, clumsy, utterly adorable. She knelt down and was engulfed in puppy love: soft, wet, warm, *unconditional*. It felt wonderful.

"Stop fraternizing with the talent," Marc Tanner called to her from across his studio.

"They started it," Avery said as the dogs' trainer came over and lured the puppies back to the kitchen set.

Avery and Justin had just arrived at Marc Tanner's photography studio for a meeting about the perfume campaign and launch. The studio was in a converted nineteenth-century carriage house not far from Flair's office. A team from Flair's advertising agency was also there.

Marc was one of the city's most successful photographers. He was famous for his brilliant "eye," but was also sought-after for his big-picture talents. He had the ability to envision and articulate an overall look and style for a product. Marc was going to be shooting the perfume's print campaign, and Avery wanted his input on the design and image they would be creating.

"We're just about wrapped up here, give me ten minutes," Marc said. He was in his late thirties, tall and lean, strikingly handsome with angular features.

Justin and Avery watched as Marc confidently shot the puppies devouring their food. He worked quickly and was filled with kinetic energy. To capture different angles, he knelt, lay on the floor, climbed a ladder—click click, click click. Avery felt her blood course a little faster.

True to his prediction, Marc finished up in no time. As the puppies' trainer packed them into crates, Marc led everyone to his upstairs office. The walls were covered with shots of celebrities and stills from ad campaigns he had worked on. They all sat around an enormous table, except Marc, who paced like a panther. "So, tell me where you are with the perfume," he said.

Avery loved Marc's energy, the way he cut to the heart of the matter. It made her step up her own game.

"Justin and I are going to Paris next week, we're going to work with a master perfumer to create the scent. The name is still up in the air, and we're in the early stages of formulating the look, the tone, the copy. We wanted to bring you in early in the process. I know I want something sensual and romantic, as opposed to overtly sexual."

"Okay, just off the top of my head: you want a defining look—something striking that burns your brand into consumers' consciousness. There's so much clutter out there, I'd think simple—clean, clear lines. Nothing heavy. The perfume is aimed at young women, right?"

"Yes," Avery said.

"And it will be reasonably priced?"

"Yes."

"Okay . . . nature, the elements . . . *rain!* Rain is romantic. Water is sensual."

"Water is all wet," Parker pronounced, striding into the room. All heads turned. "And it's soggy; it has no drama, no excitement. How about *Neon*—it's flashy, electric, provocative."

Avery looked at Parker and tried to contain her shock. She was wearing an understated navy suit with a white blouse. Her makeup was subtle, her hair was soft and simple, and she was wearing glasses. Parker looked almost demure, like a serious young businesswoman. But it was all so clearly an act.

Avery felt the back of her neck flush red. She stood, crossed to Parker, and lowered her voice, "I'd like to talk to you alone." Then she led her out into the hallway, out of earshot.

"What kind of stunt are you trying to pull here?" she demanded.

"It's not a stunt. It's called having input on a company I own."

"A company I founded and I run."

"Why didn't you tell me about this meeting?" Parker challenged.

"Because I knew you'd have nothing to offer but a lot of tacky ideas."

Avery couldn't believe that Parker had shown up in that costume, waltzed into the meeting, tried to take over and ram her agenda down everyone's throat. It was the amateur hour. And it was a naked power play. She took Parker by the elbow and led her to a small alcove.

"Listen, Parker, Flair is built on *my* vision and *my* sweat. I'm running the show."

"Actually, you're not."

"You're acting like a spoiled, entitled little brat," Avery said.

"Well, guess what, this little brat owns fifty-one percent of Flair."

"You want to buy me out?" Avery dared. "Well, do you? Because it's fine with me. You can buy me out and I'll take my money and start a new company. And I guarantee you that within a year, you will have run Flair into the ground!"

Parker blinked—and for a split second uncertainty flashed in her eyes.

"You wouldn't do that," she said, but her voice had lost its confidence.

"You push me too hard, Parker, and I sure as hell will. I'm sick of your threats."

Parker turned away from her, sat in a nearby chair, smoothed out her skirt and hair, adjusted her glasses. When she looked up at Avery her tone had changed, softened. "I came here today because I want to be part of things, Avery. I want to be taken seriously. I don't want to spend the rest of my life partying and shopping. That's why I dressed like this, to prove to you that I'm trying to change. I've been clean and sober for six days. I've been going to meetings. Please give me a chance, please . . ."

Parker's eyes welled with tears, and for a moment Avery saw Finn in those eyes. She remembered how worried he had been about Parker, how much he loved his baby girl. Avery took a deep breath. She owed it to Finn to give Parker another chance.

"I'm sorry if I act like a spoiled brat sometimes," Parker said, fighting down tears. "I really am. You know, I'm pretty much all alone in the world. My mother and I talk maybe once every two months. The only thing she cares about is seeing herself in the pages of *Town & Country*. And my dad is dead. But nobody has any sympathy because I'm rich. Well, I didn't ask to be rich." Parker took off her glasses and wiped at her eyes. "I want to be part of Flair, Avery. I admire you so much. Want to hear something really funny? I'm jealous of *you*. I really am. You have a purpose in life, a *passion*. I want that, I want it so badly."

It was true that Parker hadn't had an easy life, in spite of her money and privilege. Ironically, in fact, in some ways she was a victim of them. And she was just a kid. What kid doesn't make mistakes? Maybe she really was trying to change, trying to pull herself together. Most important, she was Finn's daughter. And Avery would love Finn Adams until the day she died.

"Listen, Parker, why don't we go back into the meeting and start over? But if you want to be part of my team, you have to be a team player."

"Oh, Avery, thank you." She reached out and took Avery's hand. "Friends?"

"Friendship has to be earned, Parker," Avery said. "Now, come on, we've got work to do."

13

IT WAS JUST before eight o'clock that night and Avery was at her desk, going over a list of department stores that might be convinced to stock Flair products. What she was really doing was trying to contain her excitement as she waited for Lucy Charles to arrive.

The rest of the meeting with Marc Tanner had gone well. They'd come up with a concept for the perfume: scent as a pathway to the heart. The trip to Paris to create the fragrance was the next step. Parker had shown flashes of petulance, but all in all had behaved pretty well. Avery hoped that she was sincere about wanting to change. Because of Finn, Avery was willing to give her the benefit of the doubt. For the moment.

Avery stood up and went to the window. The lights of Manhattan glittered outside. The view never failed to give her an adrenaline rush. And she was going to need all the adrenaline she could muster. In addition to the perfume, Avery had to stay on top of the rest of Flair. Even with Justin, there just weren't enough hours in the day. She realized that what she needed was an assistant dedicated solely to the perfume. The launch party alone was a major undertaking. There were a thousand details and she wanted to stay focused on the big issues.

Avery felt that familiar tension knot laying claim to her shoulders. She rubbed the back of her neck. There was so much happening in her life, both professionally and personally. She longed for intimacy, tenderness, to be held and loved. She thought of Marcus, how understanding he could be, the way he cocked his head when he was listening to her, brushed her hair from her face, trailed his fingertips along the curve of her hip . . .

"You look like you're deep in thought," came the voice from behind her.

Avery turned from the window. The young woman standing in her doorway was in her early twenties, quite chubby, with brown hair pulled back into a ponytail and a plain round face that radiated a quivery overeagerness. She had Patricia's green eyes, just as Avery did.

"Lucy?"

"Avery?"

They looked at each other across the expanse of the office for a long suspended moment. Then they rushed together and hugged, laughing. When they broke, Avery held Lucy at arm's length, beaming.

"Well, sister . . . ," Avery said.

"You're so pretty," Lucy said, and then she looked down, embarrassed.

". . . And you're adorable."

"Could I get that in writing?"

Lucy's striped sundress was old-fashioned and didn't fit very well. She was wearing expensive flats, but they were scuffed up. Lucy was clearly uncomfortable in her own body, and Avery felt badly for her and was touched by her vulnerability.

"This is very exciting for me. I've always wanted a sister," Avery said.

"Me, too."

"Am I your only sibling?"

"Unless you want to count some steps I never see."

In spite of her insecurities, Lucy's speech made it clear that she'd gone to good schools. Avery liked the idea of having a sister who was well educated and well spoken. It was another piece in the new sense of herself that she was developing after learning the truth of her birth and parentage. She had a famous mother and a sister who went to private schools. She was more than just a girl from the wrong side of the tracks in Wilkes-Barre.

"Boy, this place is cool," Lucy said, looking around. Avery's office was furnished with clean, stylish elegance.

"It's important to keep up appearances in this business. Flair is doing well, but expenses are very high. We're still in the plow-every-dime-back-into-the-company phase. I keep my own salary low. Of course, if . . . I mean *when* we really take off, I'll be a rich woman," Avery said.

"Mom told me you founded the company."

"Yes, I did. In my kitchen, believe it or not."

"Okay, I officially hate you. Hey, I was president of the French Club in college."

"Well then, we're even. I am so bad with languages."

They smiled at each other, an easy smile.

"Dinner?" Avery asked.

"Before we go, I'd love a little tour."

Avery spent the next half hour showing Lucy around Flair. They'd kept the old warehouse space mostly open, and all the employees were encouraged to personalize their individual work areas. Avery liked to create an atmosphere of creative cross-pollination. There was the lab where new products were formulated, meeting rooms and offices, a kitchen, a small gym, and a child-care center.

"It's crucial to have all of the amenities that we do; it's the only way we can attract top talent. It's expensive, but worth it," Avery explained.

"I read an article about Flair online that said it was a fantastic place to work," Lucy said.

"We try. I can be tough, but I hope I'm fair. There are always issues, but knock wood."

"Well, I'm so impressed . . . and proud of you."

Lucy's eyes were filled with respect. Avery had a sister, a bright, wonderful, kind sister. She felt her throat tighten, and was embarrassed by her emotion.

"I mean this place is just amazing, and to think you did it all from scratch. I have a billion and one questions, so if I get to be too much just tell me to shut up."

"Hey, what are big sisters for?"

"I know you're developing a perfume. That is so cool. I want to hear all about it."

Avery was charmed by Lucy's lack of cynicism, by her almost naïve enthusiasm and curiosity. What a refreshing contrast with Patricia Lucas's artifice and manipulation. Unlike Patricia, Avery felt immediately that she could trust Lucy, that there was no hidden agenda. As they headed out to the elevator, she thought: this is one apple that fell pretty far from the tree.

14

AVERY AND LUCY cabbed uptown to a restaurant across from Lincoln Center. It was a see-and-be-seen kind of place that Avery thought Lucy would enjoy. They ordered salads, pasta, white wine. The wine arrived and they raised their glasses.

"To sisterhood," Avery toasted.

They clinked and sipped.

"All right, start talking," she said.

"Cliff Notes version: birth, grade school, folks divorce, Dad re-marries, Mom remarries, high school, Mom remarries again, col-lege, move to New York, meet sister, sip wine. End of story," Lucy said.

"Not so fast—beginning of story. What does your dad do?"

"He was a movie producer. But he was smart enough to get out of the business. Now he and his wife own an eco-resort in Costa Rica."

"And you grew up in Los Angeles?" Avery asked.

"Yes, Beverly Hills."

"Did you know Parker Adams by any chance?"

"*Everyone* knows Parker Adams. We both went to the Westlake School, but she was a few years ahead of me. You know her?"

"She's a partner in Flair."

"No kidding, small world. How did that happen?"

"She inherited a stake from her dad when he died," Avery said.

"Is she still as wild?"

"Yes. Well, *maybe* not. She's trying to reform."

"Good. There's nothing more pathetic than an aging bad girl," Lucy said.

"What about . . . Patricia?" Avery asked.

"Still hard for you to call her Mom?"

"I've barely known her for a week," Avery said. "Besides, I don't know if I'll ever think of her as my mom. But I'm very curious: what was she like as a mother?"

"Well, she's an actress, and actress and mom don't belong in the same sentence. She's a good actress, she's sensitive, but self-absorbed. I was left alone a lot growing up. We had a big house, but it was a pretty lonely place for me," Lucy said, and a look of sadness swept across her face. Avery imagined that it must be hard to have a mother as beautiful and graceful as Patricia, especially when you're overweight and a little clumsy.

"And what about the two stepfathers?"

"When Mom fell in love, she just disappeared. To Big Sur, Hawaii, Baja—half the time I didn't even know where. Then suddenly a new man would move into the house. The first stepdad was a creep, but he was rich and Mom's career was stalled, so I think he represented security. He barely lasted a year. Number two was a real sweetheart. He was a cinematographer, charming and fun. Those were wonderful years. But then he left her, and I don't think Mom has ever really recovered."

"And she never ever mentioned me?" Avery asked, even though she knew the answer.

Lucy looked into Avery's eyes for a moment. Then she looked down and said, "I'm sorry."

"Out of sight, out of mind," Avery said, trying to sound casual but hearing the catch in her voice.

"I think it's much more complicated than that. When Mom finally told me about you last month, she said that she always felt like there was a hole in her life, in her heart, and that she would never feel peace until she found you. I think she feels tremendous guilt about what she did," Lucy said.

Good, Avery thought.

"How do you feel about her?" Lucy asked.

Their salads arrived. Avery took a bite and then said, "I'm glad I know the truth."

"That doesn't answer my question," Lucy said.

"I feel like I need a little more time to sort out my feelings. Does that sound like a cop-out?"

"No, I'm sure it's very complicated for you," Lucy said. "Now, how about you? Tell me something about Avery."

"What would you like to know?" Avery asked.

"Where did you grow up? Any siblings?"

"I grew up in Wilkes-Barre, Pennsylvania . . . very middle class, ordinary, no siblings." Part of her wished she could tell Lucy the truth, but she couldn't bring herself to do it. Her secret was too shameful. Revealing it would be revealing a weakness. Finn was the only person she had ever felt safe telling.

"What about your adoptive parents, what are they like?"

"They're divorced. My mom has Alzheimer's and lives in a group home. Dad lives in Texas. We're not that close. All in all, it was hardly the glamorous childhood that you had."

"Well, you're making up for it with your glamorous adulthood," Lucy said.

"Believe me, it's one percent glamour, ninety-nine percent perspiration."

"I don't see any sweat stains."

"That's the real art."

Lucy raised her glass again. "To my amazing big sister." They clinked glasses and sipped. "I mean it, Avery, I'm just in awe of you. And even though we barely know each other, I'm so proud of you."

"It means a lot to hear that from my sister."

"Although I do wish you weren't so pretty."

"Oh, Lucy, you're very attractive." When the time was right, Avery would make some suggestions on Lucy's wardrobe, treat her to a gym membership, and teach her a few makeup tricks. "Now tell me more, what are you doing in New York?"

"I just graduated from Middlebury College. Me and two friends from school have rented an apartment in Williamsburg."

"And you're going to spend the summer hanging out?"

"Hanging out my résumé . . . hint-hint."

"You didn't tell me you were looking for a job."

"Recent college grad, first apartment . . . *duh?*"

Avery laughed.

"I'll do a summer internship," Lucy said. "Nominal salary, will take lunch orders. How's that for begging?"

"Are you interested in the cosmetics business?"

"Probably not as much as I should be."

"I am looking for an assistant for the perfume launch."

"I smell hope."

"I'm going to tell you right off the bat—if I give you a job, you have to earn the right to keep it," Avery said.

"I wouldn't want it any other way."

The deal was sealed. Lucy would start work the following Monday.

15

AFTER DINNER, LUCY hopped on the subway back out to Brooklyn. Avery stood on the sidewalk. All around her well-dressed couples were laughing, holding hands, whispering intimacies. Avery felt an intense stab of loneliness that washed over her like a black wave. What good was it all—success, work, even a brand-new sister—if she didn't have someone to share it with? She pulled out her phone and dialed.

"Hello?"

"Hi, Marcus, it's me."

"Well, hi there, stranger."

"How are you?" Avery asked.

"I'm frazzled. Week from hell. What about you?" Marcus asked.

"I'm good . . . well, *pretty* good."

"What's going on?"

"Too much," Avery said, dropping her voice, hoping he would hear her need.

"You do sound a little ragged."

There was a pause. Why wasn't he happier to hear from her? Why hadn't he asked her over?

"So, where are you?" Marcus asked finally.

"Standing on the corner of Sixty-sixth and Broadway."

"Just watching the world go by?"

"Marcus, I'm lonely, can I come over?"

"Yeah, okay, sure."

It took Avery less than fifteen minutes to get over to Marcus's apartment. He lived across town in the east sixties, in a glitzy new tower. Avery could feel her want growing as the elevator raced to the thirty-second floor.

Marcus opened the door wearing beat-up jeans slung low on his hips and a wrinkled white oxford shirt. He looked a little tired, but the lines around his eyes only made him sexier. "Hey there," he said.

And then Avery was in his arms and they kissed, long and deep. He kicked the door shut behind them. They leaned against the wall and his hands ran down her back, the curve of her hips. Avery put her arms around his neck and pulled him close, inhaling the smell of his minty soap.

Marcus moved his hands up under her sweater. She wanted this, yes, but more than anything she needed to be held and loved.

"Please, let's slow down," Avery whispered.

Marcus cocked his head, puzzled, then gave a little shrug. "Sure, baby, of course."

He took her hand and led her into the apartment. His décor was definitely "guy." There were low-slung leather couches, mood lighting, and a TV the size of Rhode Island. The place looked messier than usual, with papers strewn across the floor. On a side table Avery noticed an empty champagne bottle and two flutes.

"Sorry about the mess, I wasn't expecting company," Marcus said. "I'm working on a segment on the Staten Island serial killer, and I feel like I'm his latest victim. How about a glass of wine?"

"No, thanks," Avery murmured. She led Marcus into the bedroom. She slipped off her shoes and lay on the bed. Did the pillow smell faintly of perfume, or was that just his soap?

Marcus dimmed the lights and lay beside her. He kissed her, more gently this time. "You do need some loving, don't you?" he asked, looking in her eyes.

She nodded. "I've missed you . . ."

Now they were both naked. Avery closed her eyes and gave herself over to his touch, to his large strong hands. Sometimes she was greedy in bed. This time she needed to be made love to, to feel wanted, treasured.

Marcus kissed her neck, her breasts, worked his way slowly down her body with his lips and tongue. Avery felt her skin flush with desire.

But something was wrong . . .

Marcus was distracted.

Yes, his lips were warm, his tongue exciting, but she could sense that his passion was forced. He was going through the motions and making the right moves, but there could be no doubt: he didn't need her in the same way she needed him. His body was in the bed, but his head—and probably his heart—were somewhere else.

Avery was pulled out of the moment. The spell was broken. She needed to feel cared for, desired, loved.

"Marcus?"

"Yeah?" he answered, running his fingertips gently up her inner thighs.

Avery felt a tremor of want ripple through her body and she made a decision. "Oh, nothing," she murmured. Then she opened herself up to Marcus, reached down and guided his lips to the heart of her want, arched her back, and gave herself over to pure obliterating sensation. . . .

When she was a very little girl, guided by her fierce instinct for survival, Avery had learned how to turn her pain into strength. When you're alone in a big uncaring world, selfishness isn't a vice, it's a necessity.

Early on, Avery learned how to take.

And so, in bed with Marcus, Avery got what she wanted.

What she needed would have to wait.

16

AVERY FELT LIKE she had stepped into a dream.

She was walking along the sparkling Seine. The ornate grandeur of the Hôtel de Ville was on her right, and the spire of Notre Dame was visible on the Île de la Cité just across the river. Soft puffy clouds skittered across the blue sky, bursting red geraniums overflowed their window boxes, and under café awnings people talked and laughed and watched the world go by. Avery had never seen anything as beautiful in her life, and an electric charge of pure exhilaration ran through her.

"Am I too old to skip?" she asked Justin, slipping her arm through his.

"Yes," he said, "except in Paris."

And so skip they did. It was giddy and glorious, and they finally collapsed against each other, laughter pealing.

The whole day was like that, as Justin showed Avery his adored city. They laughed, ran, sang, and strolled through the Luxembourg Garden, where boys in shorts sailed tiny boats on the pond and a bosky grotto felt like a secret world; along the narrow streets of the Marais, a surprise around every corner; up and down the cobbled pathways of Père Lachaise Cemetery, where the grave of Oscar Wilde sported a single red rose; past chic shops and legendary cafés along the Boulevard St. Germain; and finally to the Eiffel Tower just as soft dusk descended on the City of Light.

Avery had seen a thousand images of the tower. Who hasn't? But nothing prepared her for the scale, the wonder, the sheer piercing beauty of Monsieur Eiffel's glorious folly.

She and Justin rode the elevator to the top. They stood on the balcony looking out at the ancient and majestic city, blue gray in the twinkling twilight.

"Thank you for this," Avery said simply.

"I don't think I've ever seen you this happy," Justin said.

"I don't think I've ever *been* this happy."

"It's good for the soul, isn't it?" Justin said.

"Yes, and it's just what I need."

"At some point in life, everyone needs Paris. . . . Oh dear, I'm afraid that sounded a bit pretentious."

"Oh, who gives a damn if it did? I loved the way it sounded and I think Justin Fowler is a dear heart and a dear friend," Avery said, kissing him on the cheek.

"You're a very easy person to be a friend to, Avery," Justin said, his voice growing serious. "And although you never talk about them, I know you've had your struggles."

"Don't you think everyone struggles, at some time?" Avery asked.

"I do, but some struggle more than others, and do it with grace and not a trace of self-pity. I'd put you in that category." Justin looked out at the view, and then down at his hands, as if memories were flooding over him. He swallowed and sadness came into his eyes. He rarely spoke of his personal life with Avery, and now she sensed he wanted to.

"I'm also a good listener," Avery said, leaning her shoulder into his.

Justin looked out again and began to speak, slowly, softly, "Neal and I stood in almost this exact spot, just a month before he died. Oh, you would have adored Neal, Avery, and he would have adored you. He was smart and funny, but more than all that, he was kind. We'd been together for ten years and then he got sick. His last wish was to come back to Paris, where we'd spent so much time together. He was weak, but so determined. We had a tender, heartbreaking week . . . and when we got home, he slipped into a coma. . . . Paris was our last memory. . . ."

Avery was moved and felt privileged to hear this. She had known about Neal, but not the details of his last days. Then her heart turned to memories of Finn Adams, the love of her life. Also gone forever. She rested her head on Justin's shoulder. Her eyes welled with tears.

Night had fallen on the city and there was nothing more to say.

17

THEIR HOTEL WAS on the Left Bank, near
the church and square of St. Sulpice. It was small
and charming, housed in a former abbey, and had a lovely garden in
the back. Avery and Justin ate their breakfast in the garden. They
were surrounded by birdsong and the intoxicating smells of fresh
baked bread, strong coffee, and flowering mimosa and jasmine.

"Paris smells different from New York, doesn't it?" Avery said.
"These croissants, for instance, don't smell like New York croissants."

"They certainly don't. They smell heavenly—so heavenly in fact
that I'm going to throw fat grams to the wind," Justin said, slather-
ing a croissant with butter and jam and taking an enormous bite.
"P.S.—they don't *taste* like New York croissants either."

"Isn't it incredible, the way all these smells are affecting our spirits right now?" Avery asked. She brought a small cup of lemon mar-
malade up under her nose and savored its sweet piquancy.

"Fragrance is one of life's most delicious pleasures," Justin said.
"And today is our day of scents. Our appointment with Henri Bihary
is in the afternoon, but this morning I want to show you my favorite

Parisian perfume shop. It is a store like nothing we'd ever find in New York."

And so they set off on foot for an out-of-the-way corner of the Right Bank. Set in the crook of a small street, DeLuc had a modest storefront with a dusty array of bottles arranged in its front windows. A hand-painted sign announced that it had been founded in 1892.

As they opened the door, a bell tinkled softly to announce their arrival. Avery felt like she was stepping into the past. The store was compact and had an authentic patina. There were carved wood accents, a writing desk, and two walls of mirrored shelves filled with graceful bottles of perfume, eau de cologne, and eau de toilette. The smell in the shop, the mingling of a century's worth of fragrances, was surprisingly light and fresh.

A woman of about fifty appeared from the back. She was a bit stout, her hair was pinned up, and she was nicely dressed in a matching gray skirt and sweater. Her practical manner was softened by the warm twinkle in her eye.

"Bonjour, mademoiselle, monsieur," she said.

"Bonjour," Avery said.

"Is there something that I may help you with?" the woman asked.

"We'd like to look around, if we may," Justin said.

"But of course," the woman said.

Avery walked over to the shelf and admired the bottles. They were graceful and timeless, with gold caps, and the lettering on the labels was feminine and cursive. She opened the one called Les Fleurs Secrete and then took one of the small paper blotters out of its glass holder. She sprayed the blotter with a shot of the perfume and then held it under her nose. A heady bouquet excited her senses.

"Mademoiselle has wonderful taste. Les Fleurs Secrete is our most popular fragrance. It contains rose, jasmine, lavender, and berg-amot. Lovely, no?"

"Delicious," Avery said, holding the blotter under Justin's nose.

"Divine," he agreed.

"It was Countess DeLuc's original fragrance in 1892. She couldn't find a perfume that suited her mood in the spring, on spring evenings to be exact. And so she contracted with the most fa-mous perfumer of the day and they created Les Fleurs Secrete. All of the countess's friends loved the way it smelled when she wore it and they wanted the perfume for themselves, and so then she went into business."

Avery noticed framed letters hanging on the walls. Many were yellowed with age.

"Yes, you see the letters from her customers. This one is from the queen of Belgium. And here is one from the crown princess of Bul-garia. And the maharajah of Jaipur. This letter is from Lillie Langtry, the most famous actress of the time."

"Can you translate this one for me?" Avery asked, pointing to the letter from the queen of Belgium, handwritten on heavy royal sta-tionery.

"With pleasure," the woman said. She read: "To my dear Count-ess, La Mer Vetiver is so lovely. I find myself wearing nothing else these days, and people smile at me in appreciation. I look forward to seeing you when I am next in Paris, and in the meantime would you be so kind as to send along two bottles. You have made me very happy. Warmest wishes."

"Oh, Justin, don't you feel like this is living history?" Avery asked.

"It *is* living history," he answered.

Avery lowered her voice. "But do you think maybe these scents are a little too old-fashioned for Flair?"

Just then a Mercedes sedan pulled up in front of the shop. The driver got out and opened the rear door. A beautiful young woman, looking chic yet casual in slacks and an exquisite purple silk blouse, stepped out of the car. She walked into the shop and exchanged greetings with the proprietress. The older woman handed her a small package and she turned and left.

"Who was that?" Justin asked.

"Dominique Beauvoir, a very popular film actress," she told him. "She wears only DeLuc."

"I think I just learned an important lesson," Avery said. She turned to the woman. "I'll take a bottle of Les Fleurs Secrete, please."

"Of course."

From DeLuc, Avery and Justin walked farther north. They reached a working-class neighborhood that was home to apartment blocks, old lofts, and small factories.

"Here we are," Justin announced when they were in front of a four-story red-brick loft building. They rode up to the top floor in the large old elevator, and walked down the hall. They came to a glass-front door marked simply "Henri Bihary." Justin knocked.

A few moments later the door was opened by a middle-aged man with a fleshy face and sad tired eyes. He smelled faintly of cigarettes. "You are Justin Fowler and Avery Wilkins, I am presuming," he said in a voice that was as world-weary as his eyes.

"Yes," Justin said. "And you are Monsieur Bihary."

"Come in," Bihary said, standing aside and making a courtly gesture of welcome.

They stepped into an office that was lined with books. The windows were grimy, and papers were strewn all over the large desk. There were two old leather armchairs in one corner. Classical music was playing softly. The place felt more like the refuge of an old college professor than the inner sanctum of a man who had one of the best "noses" in the world.

"Please, sit," Bihary said, indicating the armchairs. Then he went to a hotplate and turned on the burner under a kettle.

"I thought we will have a cup of tea and talk, then we go into my lab and begin our work," he said. He picked up a small tin and opened the lid. He crossed over to Avery and held it under her nose. She inhaled the deep, full fragrance of a strong black tea.

"Mmmmm," she said.

"Tea from the Assam state in India." He held the tin under Justin's appreciative nose. Then he opened a second tin, which contained bits of dried orange rind, and a third, which held dried jasmine flowers. He held each one out for Avery and Justin to smell. Then he spooned Assam tea, orange rind, and jasmine into a teapot and added boiling water.

As they waited for the tea to brew, they listened to the symphony, coming from a small old radio on the windowsill. Avery sensed that Monsieur Bihary was orchestrating this experience, and she was content to put herself into his hands.

After a few minutes, he poured three cups of the tea, handed one to each to his guests, and sat on a stool near them. Avery brought the cup up to her face and inhaled.

"Ah, yes, Avery. You see, what minutes ago were three very different smells, have now become one. This is the magic of alchemy—blending and merging different elements to create something new and marvelous. Alchemy is the very essence of the art of perfume making. Now taste your tea, please."

Avery sipped.

"First you taste the Assam tea, no? It reaches out and grabs you, strong and bold, but then graciously steps back to let its compatriots have their say," he said. "The orange asserts itself, comes up from underneath, bitter and bracing, but courtly, with a little smile. And finally, the gentle jasmine calls to you, like a friend from across a meadow."

Avery exchanged an excited glance with Justin.

"The perfume we will be making, it is for you, yes, Avery?"

"For my company," she answered. "But, yes, for me."

"Then I must know you. I find you already *sympathique*, but I want to know more. May I ask you some questions?"

"Of course," Avery said.

"I think I should leave the two of you alone," Justin said, standing. "Avery, I'll see you back at the hotel this evening. Monsieur Bihary, I thank you so much."

Justin left and Bihary moved to the chair across from Avery. He leaned back, his hands resting on his belly, fingers entwined, and looked at her with his heavy, hooded eyes.

"I will ask you some questions, and please answer without thinking, yes?"

"Of course."

"Can you tell me please—do you prefer the night or the day?"

"I like them both, but I guess if I had to choose it would be day."

"What time of the day?"

"Early morning and evening at twilight."

"And do you prefer to be indoors or outdoors?"

"It depends on my mood, what I'm doing, and, of course, who I'm with. I'm at my happiest when I'm with someone special, no matter where we are."

"Can you tell me your favorite texture?"

"I love the feel of old wood, smooth and strong. And velvet, soft and soothing."

"And your favorite color?"

"Blue, a vibrant blue. . . ."

Bihary asked Avery about her favorite foods, landscapes, and season. He asked what excited her, what made her sad, and what she dreamed about at night. He listened intently, nodding occasionally. When he was done with his questions, he sat quietly, sipping his tea, narrowing his eyes, and observing Avery. Even under his scrutiny, she felt unself-conscious, open to the experience.

"Now . . . ," he said finally, "let us move into my laboratory."

Avery followed him into a spacious, high-ceilinged room. There was a wall of metal mullioned windows that looked out at a motley view of small factories and high-rise housing projects. There was a large center island covered with small vials, each neatly labeled and sitting on its own tiny stand. Elsewhere there was a large refrigerator and lots of built-in cabinets. The room was quiet as a church, and the sky was gray out the windows. The total effect was of a place apart, a hushed hidden world.

"This is where I work, where I perform my alchemy, where we will create a fragrance for you, Avery. Do you know much about the history of perfume?" Bihary asked.

"No, very little."

"Well, the history of man is inseparable from the history of scent. The earliest trade routes developed in search of ingredients for perfume. Ships and caravans traveled across seas and continents to the most remote corners of the earth." All the exhaustion had disappeared from Bihary's face and eyes; he moved with a new lightness and energy, and his voice was resonant and passionate. "The very first perfumers were Egyptian priests. They extracted juices from flowers and plants to create incense that they used in their ceremonies and to anoint their worshipers."

Avery was mesmerized.

"When Moses and the Jews returned to Jerusalem from exile in

Egypt, they brought these early perfumes with them. In Jerusalem, archeologists discovered a primitive perfume-making laboratory that dates back to before Christ."

"Amazing," Avery said.

"By the time of the Roman Empire, the use of scent was common. Wealthy Romans would release scented doves at their bacchanals. They also brushed the walls of their villas with flower essences, and spread petals across the floors of their boudoirs and bathing rooms."

Bihary gestured to the table, with its kingdom of bottles and vials. "The early perfumers were true alchemists. They transformed physical matter into divine essence, into spirit and soul. They were considered magicians able to inspire great thinkers, heal the sick, and of course excite lovers to new heights of passion. By the Middle Ages, there were perfumers throughout Europe."

"But these perfumes must have been very expensive. Were they just for the rich?" Avery asked.

"In large part, yes. Then, in the late nineteenth century, synthetic essences were created. This meant lower costs, and perfume became a luxury that many women could afford."

"But are synthetics really as good as pure essences?" Avery asked.

"Unless you want to charge five hundred dollars for your perfume, I would say they are as good," Bihary said with a knowing smile.

"Point taken," Avery said.

"I am an artisan, but I am also a professional. And many synthetics today are of wonderful quality. And, of course, some ingredients are very hard to come by in their natural state. Do you know about musk?"

"I know it originally came from the musk deer, that's about it."

"Yes, and the musk deer live only in the Himalayan Mountains, and only the males have the musk gland. They must be killed to extract the gland, and sadly they have been hunted almost to extinction. Musk is perhaps the most powerful and long-lasting of all scents. There are ancient mosques in the Middle East that had musk glands mixed with their mortar, and a thousand years later the scent is still perceptible! With so few musk deer left, it is hardly practical, but the synthetics are a worthy substitute."

Bihary unstopped a vial, dipped in a dipstick, and waved it under Avery's nose. The smell was dense, dusky, animalistic. Avery thought of ancient forests, dappled sunlight, passion, and desire.

"Intense," Avery said.

"Yes. And it is synthetic musk. It must be used sparingly. Too much of any one thing is rarely good in a perfume. Think that you are an orchestra conductor, Avery, creating a symphony of scent, working not with musical notes and instruments, but smells. Do you know the building blocks of a perfume?"

"I have some ideas, but I'd rather hear them from you," Avery said.

"Ah! A good pupil knows when to flatter the teacher. There is the top, or head, note. This is the note that dominates on first smelling a perfume, and it is the note that dissipates the most quickly. Then the middle, or heart, note is revealed. The heart note will linger for a while, and it links the top and base. Finally you have the base note, which is revealed last and remains the longest. Can you tell me which kind of note musk is?"

"It would have to be a base note."

"Yes, of course. Some perfumers start with the top note and work down to the base. I like to move from the bottom up. But, enough talk." Bihary picked up a small glass beaker from the counter. "Are you ready to get to work?"

"Yes, sir," Avery answered, a tingle racing up her spine.

As they worked the hours passed and Avery lost track of time, lost herself in the magic of creation, forgot all about the world out the window, forgot about Parker and Patricia and Marcus; there was only this, *the work*. Although once, when she looked up at the darkening Paris sky, she felt a soft stab of yearning for Finn Adams.

18

IT WAS EARLY evening when Avery finally left Bihary's atelier. She was exhausted but exhilarated, and carried a small bottle of the prototype of her perfume safely in her bag. She had learned so much today, about the history and techniques of perfume making, but also about respecting your work and honoring the past. As she passed the Place de la Bastille with its modern Opera House and headed toward the Seine, she felt a contented fatigue.

It was a misty evening and halos glowed around the streetlights. Up ahead was the river, and in the middle of it was the Ile St. Louis, its tip looking like the prow of a ship. A sudden wave of loneliness swept across Avery. In her head she knew she was an independent woman forging a successful career, but in her heart she yearned, desperately, for someone to be with at the end of the day.

Avery reached the Seine and crossed over to the Ile St. Louis, heading to the Left Bank and the hotel. The narrow island came to a tapered point and there was a small park on the tip. She stood looking out at the swirling waters. The beauty of the island assuaged her loneliness, transformed it into a bittersweet melancholy. As she turned from the park she saw a figure coming toward her, a man.

"Avery?"

". . . Brad Henry!?" she gasped.

He laughed and said, "*Bonsoir.*" Then he kissed her in the French fashion, first on one cheek and then the other. He was wearing corduroy pants, a blue oxford shirt, and a dark blazer, and looked relaxed and handsome, completely at home in Paris.

"This is certainly a big surprise," she said, ". . . but a nice one. What are you doing in Paris?"

"Want to take a little walk and I'll tell you all about it?"

They began to stroll around the perimeter of the Ile St. Louis. The river was on one side of them, and gracious limestone mansions and apartment houses were on the other. They walked in silence for a few moments, their shoulders occasionally touching.

"So, how is everything going here?" Brad asked.

"It's going well, very well. I met with a master perfumer today and we . . . Wait, weren't you going to tell me what *you're* doing in Paris?"

"Actually, I followed a woman here."

"Oh . . . ?"

"She's a very special woman, and even though we don't know each other all that well, I couldn't stop thinking about her, wanting to be with her. And so I hopped on a plane, went to her hotel, was informed by her colleague of her likely route home . . . ," Brad turned to Avery, ". . . and here I am."

Avery felt her heart opening like a morning rose. "Lucky girl," she said softly.

"Lucky guy."

And then they kissed. It was a light kiss, a kiss of greeting, of celebration, but it held great promise.

They walked again, now hand in hand, chatting in an easy way, but with a charged undercurrent of attraction. They found themselves in front of a small bistro. "This is one of my favorite restaurants in Paris," Brad said.

"How odd that we should land here."

"Accidents happen. You must be hungry after a long afternoon of making magic."

"Now that you mention it, I'm famished."

The inside of the restaurant was cozy, with tobacco-colored walls, maroon leather banquettes, and soft yellow lighting. They were shown to a table in the back. The waiter brought them glasses of white wine and an appetizer of salmon tartare on toast. Avery felt cosseted and safe. It was partly the restaurant, of course, but it was mostly Brad's company. There was something about his sturdy, compact body, and his confidence, understated but worldly, that made her feel protected. It was the same way she felt when she was with Finn. Under the table she slipped off her shoes and wriggled her toes.

"So, now you know the story of my appearance on the Ile St. Louis. It's your turn—tell me about your day with Monsieur Bihary," Brad said.

Avery felt a renewed surge of excitement and she began to speak quickly, passionately. "Oh, Brad, it was such an amazing experience. Making a perfume is like composing a symphony, only you use scents instead of notes."

"So tell me which notes you picked."

"Well, for my base note I chose white cedar, which has an earthy odor that's calming and an aphrodisiac, amber for a touch of sweetness, and vanilla to add a hint of memory. Then for my heart note I picked cactus blossom for its airy floral scent. Then I added star orchid and sugar cane, which have . . . Oh my God, I just realized I'm talking nonstop, yakkity-yak."

"And it's fascinating," Brad said, reaching across the table and taking her hand.

"That's nice of you to say, but I believe in conversation, not monologues."

"That's what I call manners. Whoever brought you up did a very good job," Brad said.

What would he think if he knew that she had learned her manners by watching movies, reading up on etiquette, and studying the behavior of people she considered refined? That she grew up in a house where good manners meant not polishing off the whole six-pack yourself?

"Is something wrong, Avery?"

"Oh, nothing, nothing at all. . . . I've become obsessed with scent. Do you ever wear cologne?"

"Once in a while, usually when I get it as a present."

Avery's cell phone rang.

"Excuse me, I should just check who this is," she said, taking the phone out of her purse and checking the caller ID. "It's the office in New York, I really should take it. . . . Hello?"

"Hi, Avery, it's Lucy."

"Lucy, hi."

"I hope this isn't a bad time?"

"It's fine, what's up?"

"Well, I'm learning the lay of the land here at the office, but I already got a call from *Allure*. They want to know about the perfume," Lucy said.

"We're keeping everything under tight wraps, we want to build anticipation. Just say that you have no comment."

"Maybe it would help build excitement to just give out one or two tantalizing tidbits."

"I'll tell you everything when I get back."

"Oh, okay," Lucy said, doing a poor job of disguising her disappointment. Then her voice brightened. "Guess what, I met a fella."

"Lucy, that's wonderful. Who is he?"

"His name is Karl. I think he really likes me."

Avery could hear Lucy's insecurity, and sensed that she was very inexperienced with men. "That's great, Lucy, he's a lucky guy."

"Miss you, Sis."

"I miss you, too." Avery hung up, turned off her cell phone, and asked Brad, "Where were we?"

"You were about to tell me what you picked for your top note."

"I went with bergamot. It's citrusy, bright, calming *and* stimulating. Then I added a touch of grapefruit to heighten the aroma. Finally, a drop of black currant, for a whisper of elegance and sophistication." Avery noticed a waiter, standing at a polite distance. "Oh my God, we forgot to order! In fact, I forgot I was hungry."

"So did I."

"But I guess we should eat."

"I guess."

Avery and Brad took up their menus.

"I can't wait to smell your creation," Brad said in a low voice, without looking up from his menu.

"I have a sample in my bag," Avery said, also not looking up.

"I don't want to smell it here, in a restaurant, where it will be competing with all the food smells," Brad said.

"You're right, not a good idea."

"Do you think a hotel room would be a better place?"

"It might."

"After all, it will be the first time I smell it, and first times should be special."

"Do you think so?" Avery asked.

"Very special. My hotel room is quite comfortable."

"That does sound like a lovely place for your first . . ."

"Our first . . ."

There was a pause. "I think I'm ready to order," Avery said.

"What would you like?" Brad asked.

"A taxi."

19

THEIR TAXI WHISKED them to Hôtel de Crillon, the most beautiful hotel in Paris. King Louis XV built it as a private palace in 1758 and sold it to the Count de Crillon in 1788. Members of the Crillon family lived there until 1907, when it was turned into a hotel. The magnificent limestone building had a stunning location facing the wide expanse of the Place de la Concorde and the formal Tuileries Gardens.

Crossing the sidewalk to the entrance, Avery straightened her shoulders and raised her chin, trying to pretend that she strolled into five-star hotels all the time. The lobby was a rococo fantasy, with a marble floor and gilded ceiling, manned by an army of clerks and bellhops. They passed a glowing lounge, a wood-paneled bar, and a courtyard filled with whimsical topiary and beautiful people sitting at candlelit tables. It took Avery every ounce of self-control not to gawk.

Brad's room was on the top floor. Avery felt like she was walking into an enormous upholstered jewel box. Louis XIV furniture, cozy seating, thick carpet, and endless drapes filled the room. Everything was soft and plush, with flashes of gold and gilt.

It was all so lovely and romantic, but Avery felt out of place, as if a mistake had been made and someone was going to knock on the door and tell her that girls from Wilkes-Barre weren't welcome at the Crillon. She wished Brad were staying somewhere a little less intimidating.

"Are you all right, Avery?" he asked.

"Yes . . . it's just that, well, I've never been in a hotel quite like this before."

"It's not my taste, but it's what my travel agent came up with. Last-minute bookings in Paris can be tough."

Brad took off his jacket and casually tossed it over the back of a chair. Then he ran his hands through his hair, exhaled, put his hands on his hips, looked at Avery. There was an awkward silence as a current of desire and uncertainty grew between them. Avery longed to feel his embrace, but felt a nagging insecurity. Marcus was the only man she'd been with after Finn. Brad was older, more established, and had an air of quiet sexual confidence. Why had she made that stupid remark about ordering a taxi? She was just showing off, trying to prove that she was clever and sophisticated. And look where it had gotten her. Avery took a deep breath and willed herself to relax.

"Why don't we sit down?" he said.

They sat on the sofa. The coffee table held a bottle of champagne on ice, a bowl of fruit, and a plate of chocolates. Brad deftly opened the champagne, poured two glasses, handed her one.

"To your perfume," he toasted.

They clinked glasses and sipped. Avery hated the way the bubbles tickled the back of her throat and the fumes seared her nasal passages.

"You're not a big champagne fan?" Brad said.

"I love it in theory."

"Something else, then?"

"I'm fine, really."

Another silence. She could smell a hint of pine soap on him.

"You did promise me I'd get a preview of the perfume," Brad said.

Avery was grateful for the diversion. She reached for her bag and retrieved the small bottle from the inside pocket. Smiling shyly, she held it out.

He grinned seductively and said, "I'd rather smell it on you."

"Do you know," she said, "I haven't smelled it on my skin. We worked on strips of paper and pieces of cotton."

Avery opened the bottle, turned it upside down on her fingertip, and dabbed a little on her wrists and her neck. A thrill ran up her spine; it *was* wonderful—fresh and lively at first, giving way to soft enticing florals, then the earthy warmth of white cedar. Just putting it on made Avery feel attractive . . . sexy . . .

Brad took her hand and tenderly lifted her wrist to his nose. "It's fantastic," he said, looking into her eyes.

"Do you think so?"

"Yes, I think so. It's soft and subtle, full of secrets and dark longings. It's seductive in its shy, sweet way."

"There's still work to do—you see, we have to factor in the cost of the ingredients, some modifications—"

"Avery?"

"Yes?"

"It's lovely. It's perfect."

"It will smell a little different on everyone."

"At the moment, I'm only interested in the way it smells on you."

There was another silence, and Avery was aware of how dry her mouth was.

"Should I order up some dinner from room service?" Brad asked.

"I'm not sure I could . . ."

There was a knock on the door.

Brad got up and opened the door. A middle-aged maid was standing there, holding a small pile of towels with a bottle of mineral water on top. "We're all set, thank you," he said.

"I'll take the water," Avery said.

In reaching for the water, the maid dropped the top towel. She let out an apologetic gasp. Before she could bend down, Brad had picked up the towel and refolded it.

There was something about the gesture—it was so considerate, so spontaneous, but done so matter-of-factly—that calmed Avery. What did she have to fear from Brad? Her worries were really all about herself.

He returned to the couch, sat down, and handed her the water. She set it on the coffee table, and took his hand and held it to her cheek. She closed her eyes and kissed his hand. Then she kissed it again, tasted its salty warmth.

"Thank you," she said.

"For what, Avery?"

"For the lights along the Seine. For the dinner we didn't eat." She looked into his eyes. "For the water."

He moved closer to her, reached up, slid his fingers through her hair, and cupped her head in his warm hands. His lips were on hers, rough and strong, and she could smell the starch on his shirt and the heat rising off his body.

For a minute she was worried that she was suffocating, that she couldn't catch her breath. Then she realized that wasn't it at all. For the first time in a long time, she felt protected and safe, as if she could just let go of everything—of thought, reason, time—and, simply and naturally, like the rising and falling of her heartbeats, breathe.

20

AVERY SNUGGLED AGAINST Brad, her head resting on his chest, her body exhausted and content. It was a feeling she remembered from her days with Finn Adams. Did she dare to think that maybe she had found it again?

"Well, one thing's for certain," Brad said.

"What's that?" Avery asked.

"Your perfume *works*."

And then they laughed and then they couldn't stop laughing, and it felt like they were little kids, except Avery never laughed like this when she was a little kid, and she felt buoyant, effervescent, *alive*.

Brad eventually got up and went into the bathroom. She heard the tub running, and when he came back he said, "Your bath awaits you."

The bathroom was an over-the-top oasis, the tub a cloud of rosy bubbles. Avery slid into the water up to her neck. It was liquid nirvana. She leaned her head back and looked around the room, thinking: This man stays at the Crillon the way the rest of us stay at the Comfort Inn. With a little time, I could get used to this.

Then she realized that she hadn't checked in with Justin. She picked up the phone next to the tub and dialed his cell.

"Hello."

"Hi, it's me," Avery said. "I'm sorry, I . . ."

"No apologies necessary. On the contrary."

Avery thought she detected a note of anxiety in Justin's voice.

"Is everything all right?" she asked.

"Fine. You sound *very* relaxed. I'm delighted you had a good evening."

"You're a doll," Avery said.

"I'm also a realist. And he's a dreamboat. How's the Crillon?"

"In three words: fab-u-lous."

"And it went well with Bihary?"

"*Yes!*—I can't wait for you to sample what we came up with. But can it wait until the morning?"

"Of course. Have fun, you've earned it." There was that odd note in his voice again.

"Justin, are you sure everything is okay?" There was a pause. "Come on, I need to know."

"All right. I didn't want to spoil your night, but we have a big problem."

21

 AVERY WAS OUT of the tub in a flash, an animal on high alert. "What is it?"

"Parker," Justin said.

"What did she do?"

"She tried to kill herself."

"Oh no! How?" Avery asked, slipping into a robe.

"She took a lot of pills and then she slit her wrists."

"How is she?"

"She's in critical condition."

"The poor kid," Avery said, thinking how distraught Finn would be.

"She's messed up, all right. But even at a time like this, I have to think about the company. It's my job. This thing could explode and take us down with her."

Avery couldn't switch into business mode, not yet. "How did you find out?" she asked.

"I got a call from her doctor, about twenty minutes ago. Apparently

Parker gave them you as her first contact. When they couldn't reach you, they called me."

"I turned off my cell phone hours ago."

Brad appeared in the bathroom doorway, a questioning look on his face.

"Justin, hold on a sec. . . . Brad, I just got some bad news. . . ."

Brad nodded and left, closing the door behind him.

"Do you know anything more?" Avery asked.

"She'd been out drinking and drugging last night, with some hip-hop star I've never heard of. Apparently they hit all the after-hours clubs and then at the end of the night he brushed her off and went home with another woman. She went back to her loft and . . ."

"Who discovered her?"

"That's not clear to me."

"Where is she now?"

"New York Hospital."

"I have to go see her."

"Avery, I know you're concerned about Parker personally, but I have a responsibility to the company. It's going to be impossible to keep this out of the press. And every mention of Parker Adams will mention Flair. If we were Revlon or Estée Lauder we could absorb this kind of thing, but we're a young company, still forming a public image, and notoriety like this could be fatal."

"Believe me, I'm not going to let Parker take us down. But you have to remember who her father was. Finn Adams took a chance on me. I feel like I owe him."

"I'm no fool, Avery," Justin said quietly.

"I know you're not, and I appreciate your discretion. And the cold truth is that the stronger my relationship with Parker, the better it is for Flair."

"That's true," Justin said.

"How soon can we get a flight?" Avery asked.

"I've already booked us on the first one out in the morning."

"Can we get an update on her condition?"

"Her doctor is going to call me if anything changes. Avery, we have to face the fact that she could die."

"I know that."

"That said, there isn't a damn thing we can do until tomorrow. So you may as well try and relax. We need you rested."

Avery hung up and sat on the edge of the tub. She realized how shallow her breathing was, that she was in a kind of shock. This could be a very serious setback. She tried to think through the ramifications, but she kept seeing Finn's face, filled with love as he talked about his daughter.

22

BRAD WAS SITTING on the couch, leafing through a magazine. He stood up when Avery walked into the room. She told him the news.

"Do you want me to hire a private jet?"

"That's very generous, but we're booked on the first flight to-morrow."

"In that case, I'm going to finally order up something from room service. I think you need to eat. How does an omelet and a salad sound?"

"Perfect."

He took her face in his hands and gave her a gentle kiss. "I'm sorry this had to happen."

Brad's sympathy, his offer of the plane, ordering the food—it was as if they were in this together. He was an ally, a friend as well as a lover.

Avery curled up on the sofa and watched while he talked to room service in perfect French. When he was done, he sat on the other end of the sofa and began to rub her feet.

"Unfortunately, I have to fly to Moscow tomorrow on business, so I won't be able to accompany you back to New York," Brad said. "Even more unfortunate is the fact that I have to be there for several weeks."

This was another blow. Avery had been thinking how nice it would be to have his steadying presence around. "I'll miss you."

They were silent for a little while as he ministered to her.

"Do you want to talk about Parker?" Brad asked.

Avery exhaled with a sigh. "Yes. No. I don't want to burden you with it."

"Ever heard the expression 'captive audience'?"

"I have this intense connection to her, because I was close to her father," Avery said.

"How close?"

"Close," Avery said, letting her inflection speak for itself. "*And* he capitalized my company. He died in a plane crash two years ago, and ever since I've felt responsible for Parker, like I have to watch out for her. On the other hand, she owns fifty-one percent of Flair and she's self-destructive, even dangerous. The whole relationship is incredibly complicated and a complete emotional roller coaster. She knows how to push every button I have."

"It all sounds very difficult."

"She's so manipulative. She gave the hospital my name as her primary contact. Not her mother, not a friend, but me. How is that supposed to make me feel?"

"You're obviously very important to her."

Avery reached over and fished her cell phone out of her bag. There were two messages. One was from New York Hospital. The other was from Parker's cell.

"There's a message from her," Avery said.

"Can I hear it?"

Avery nodded and put it on speakerphone.

"Hi, Avery, it's me . . . ," Parker began in a slurred, weepy voice. "I've been a bad girl, Avery, I had some drinks and some pills and stuff and now the sun is coming up and I'm *so lonely*. . . ." She started sobbing. "I'm a totally worthless fuckup, Avery, and I *hate* myself, I hate myself so much . . . but don't worry, Avery, I won't bother you anymore, I won't bother anyone anymore . . ." Parker fought down her sobs, and choked out her next words, "I want you to know something . . . I love you, I mean it, I *love* you, so please please *please* don't hate me. I can prove how much I love you, Avery. . . . I changed my will, I'm leaving you my share of Flair, it's all yours now, Avery, everything is yours. . . . I know this is what Daddy would have wanted. . . ."

And then the phone went dead.

23

AS AVERY RODE up in the elevator at New York Hospital she tried to prepare herself for seeing Parker, whose condition had been upgraded from critical to serious. Facing her wasn't going to be easy. Avery was exhausted, fighting a mean case of jet lag, and feeling very conflicted. She felt a deep empathy toward Parker, and was touched and shocked that she had changed her will. Avery kept hearing the final words in her message—*this is what Daddy would have wanted*. She needed to help Parker, both to honor Finn and also because a sane and sober Parker was in Avery and Flair's best interest. But she was also furious at her self-destructive behavior. It turned out that Parker herself had called 911. Avery suspected that the whole suicide attempt was all an act to get attention and sympathy. She was sick of putting up with Parker's bullshit. It was endangering everything Avery had worked for.

The elevator doors opened. Marcus was standing in front of her.

"Marcus . . . hi," Avery said, caught off guard.

"Hi, Avery."

Avery felt a sudden wave of guilt. She had to tell Marcus about Brad. Didn't she? Just because he had slept with another woman and wasn't going to tell her, didn't mean that she wanted to play by those same rules. Besides, her relationship with Brad felt like it could develop into something serious very quickly. Maybe it was time to end it once and for all with Marcus.

"How is Parker doing?" Avery asked.

"Not that great. In fact, I'd say she's in pretty bad shape."

"I'm sorry to hear that."

The two of them stood there for a moment in silence. Marcus looked serious and handsome, even mature. Their history together flooded back to Avery. All the wonderful times. The way Marcus had taken her by the hand and introduced her to New York City. Saturday afternoons spend visiting art galleries, performances at Carnegie Hall, those dreamy evenings out at the Brooklyn ballpark. He had been her guide, generous and exuberant, never condescending about her lack of education. Looking at him, Avery felt a yearning for what they'd had together, and sadness that it was gone.

"Listen, Avery, can we talk a minute?" Marcus said, indicating a windowed seating alcove.

Avery nodded and followed him over. They sat in two armchairs.

"I really don't know how to begin, or even what I want to say exactly," Marcus said, leaning forward on his knees, looking down at the floor, scratching his scalp. He looked up at her. "I guess I just want to say that I know we went off track somewhere and that it's probably my fault, but that I want us to try and get back on track. And I'd like to know how you feel about that."

He looked at her with real vulnerability in his eyes. She owed him honesty.

"Well, right now I'm not sure how I feel," Avery said.

"Does that mean you *don't* want to try and work things out?"

Avery didn't answer. Marcus understood what her silence meant.

"What happened?" he asked. "Is it just because I was an asshole once? . . . Oh, all right, more than once."

"No, it's not just that."

Marcus took this in. "You mean there's someone else?" he asked quietly.

Avery hesitated. It was so hard to hurt him like this. She felt like she was in suspended animation, that time had stopped. But she knew it wouldn't be fair to Marcus, to Brad, or to herself to lie. Finally she nodded.

Marcus stood up and went to the window. He stretched his arms up and grabbed the top of the frame and looked out at the city.

Avery waited, her breathing shallow.

Marcus nodded his head, slowly, bitterly. Then he swung around and spit out, "Who is he?"

Avery didn't answer.

Marcus took a few deep breaths, and asked in a calmer voice, "How long has this been going on?"

"It just started."

"Well, if it just started, it can just end." He took another deep breath. "I'm sorry, Avery, that sounded wrong. I guess I forfeited the right to tell you when to start or end anything. What I meant was, it's still in the early stages. Is that right?"

"Yes," Avery said, thinking back to last night, how wonderful Brad had been.

"So . . . you may discover that he turns into a werewolf during the full moon."

They both smiled. It was forced but it still felt good. It felt like maybe they could be friends.

"Well, I'm not giving up hope until at least the next new moon,"

Marcus said. He exhaled sharply. "Damn, do you know how painful this is for me?"

Avery felt her throat tighten. "I'm sorry."

He sat back down, looked at her. "I thought we had the real thing, Avery."

"It was real."

"*Was?*"

"Oh, Marcus, we both know that things have changed between us."

"Well, I want to get the old us back," he said.

He took her hand and entwined it with his. His hands were strong and beautiful.

"Listen, Avery, I know I should be more grown-up at thirty, but in some ways I'm still on a learning curve, especially emotionally. And I've been under so much goddamn pressure at work. You know I want to be a senior producer. Put the two things together and you have a guy who behaves in some pretty immature ways now and then. . . . All right, I'm going to shut up now. All I ask is that you not close the book on us, not yet. Can you promise me that, please?"

Avery was touched by his plea and by his admission. He was trying to grow up. She had an urge to reach out and throw her arms around him and kiss him. She was surprised by the depth of her feelings. She fought back the tears that were building in her throat.

She nodded.

Marcus brought her hand to his face and kissed it once. Then he let go and stood up. "I'll be in touch," he said. "Or you will." He walked to the elevator and pressed the button. Then he turned to Avery and said, "I hate the bastard."

The elevator arrived and he stepped on board.

Avery sat there for a moment, absolutely still. Her sadness slowly transformed into something else: a sense of power. She couldn't contain a little smile. No matter how messy and painful the details were, it was thrilling to have a man behave that way over you.

Then she got up and walked down to Parker's room.

24

PARKER LOOKED TERRIBLE. Her skin was pale and blotchy, her hair lank, her wrists were bandaged, and there were dark circles under her haunted eyes. Avery went to the bed and instinctively took her hand.

"I'm sorry," Parker said.

"I know you are," Avery said.

"I made a lot of trouble for a lot of people by acting like a spoiled, self-obsessed ten-year-old—*again*. It's just not acceptable behavior."

Avery hoped her silence made it clear that she agreed. Next to the bed there was a massive bouquet that looked like it must have cost five hundred dollars.

"My mother sent that. She's down in Palm Beach for a charity ball. She didn't bother to pick up the phone and call, but hey, you can't have everything." Silent tears began to roll down Parker's cheeks.

Nothing bugged Avery more than a pity party. Especially when the hostess was an heiress with a loft in Manhattan, a house in the

Hollywood Hills, and a body that looked great in a bikini. But Parker was Finn's kid, and that changed everything.

"I miss Daddy so much," Parker said.

Not as much as I do, Avery thought. If Finn were alive, not only would he and Avery be happily married, the two of them would be in control of the company and Parker would be nothing more than her difficult, needy stepdaughter.

"I meant what I said, Avery. I have changed my will," Parker said. "If I die, you'll inherit my share in Flair. It's what Daddy would have wanted. He always said you were very special. He said you 'had the goods,' and that was his highest compliment."

"Thank you for telling me that. And I appreciate your gesture, but I think you're going to be around for a long time."

"I don't want to live."

"You just feel that way now. You're angry at yourself for drinking and drugging, but you can go back to the meetings, get your sobriety back."

"You don't know what it's like."

"I've struggled with my own demons, Parker."

Parker ignored this admission. Avery wasn't surprised. Parker lost interest whenever she wasn't the sole topic of conversation.

Parker took a tissue from her bedside table and blew her nose. "Marcus was here."

"Yes, I ran into him in the lobby."

"He's in love with you, Avery."

"Parker, I don't think we should talk about Marcus."

"Why not?"

"Because he carries a lot of baggage for both of us."

"You don't get it, do you, Avery?"

"Get what?"

"I'm still in love with Marcus. All these other men I see are just a pathetic attempt to prove to Marcus, and to myself, that I'm over him. But I'm not and I never will be." The tears started again.

Avery's cell phone rang. She checked the incoming number. "Parker, this is the office, I should take it."

Avery walked out into the hallway, relieved for the excuse to get away from Parker and her emotional blackmail. "Hello?"

"Hi, it's Lucy." Her voice was serious and filled with sympathy. "I heard about Parker. I just want you to know how sorry I am. If there's anything I can do to make your life easier right now, just let me know."

"You don't know how good it is to hear from you. Thanks for holding down the fort."

"How are you doing, Avery?"

"I'm pretty fried, but I'm putting one foot in front of the other. Is everything going okay over there?"

"I've gotten some more calls about the perfume. Can we release any information?"

"I don't think that's a good idea. The less we tell them, the more they'll want to know," Avery said.

"Do you think we run a danger of alienating them at some point? A representative from The Tyra Banks Show told me we were acting like divas," Lucy said.

"Look who's talking."

"If you just gave me a few facts, I could dole them out very selectively."

"Experience has taught me that it's a slippery slope with the media. Give them an inch and they'll stretch it into a mile. If anyone gets peeved, tell them you're acting on direct orders from me."

There was a pause before Lucy said, "Okay. I'm sorry to bother you with all that."

"Actually, it's good to talk business in the middle of all this emotional turmoil; it helps to ground me. And Parker and Flair aren't two separate issues, as you know. I have to protect the company."

"You do an amazing job, Avery. Everyone who works here would lay down their life for you."

Avery smiled. "I hope it never comes to that, but it's nice to hear."

"Mom wanted to know if we both could come for dinner Thursday night," Lucy said.

"I'm so busy. And the whole dinner-with-Mom thing is a new concept to me."

"She's dying to see you. I think she has some news."

"All right. Tell her I'd love to."

"By the way, Sis, I had an *amazing* night last night."

"You mean . . . ?"

"Yes, with Karl. Can I tell you a really pathetic secret?" she asked excitedly.

Avery loved being the big sister. "I'm all ears."

"I had my first orgasm . . . and it was *orally induced*."

Lucy sounded like a bubbleheaded teenager and Avery had to smile. But she also realized just how immature her baby sister was. "I'm at the hospital with Parker right now," she said.

"Oh God, I'm sorry, was that an over-share? It's just that I've been *dying* tell someone about it . . ."

"I'm very happy for you, Lucy."

"Karl is so nice, Avery, he's a real gentleman."

"I can't wait to meet him. Listen, can you transfer me to Justin?"

"Of course. See you in a little while."

Avery was glad Lucy was having fun, but she was worried about her moon-eyed infatuation with this Karl. She was clearly head-over-heels, and who knew what kind of guy Karl really was. If he broke her heart it would be devastating for a girl as insecure as

Lucy. Avery felt very protective of her little sister, and decided to have a talk with her. Lucy needed to watch out for her heart.

"Hi, Avery," Justin said.

"Anything happening around there that I should know about?"

"I was just about to ask you the same question."

"Parker looks pretty bad."

"What about *you*, kiddo?"

"Hanging in."

"Well, hang tight. Listen, I'm dancing on the ceiling over this scent you came up with," Justin said with growing excitement. "I don't want to count any chickens, but I'm setting up a focus group for next week. If it goes well, I'd like to finalize the name and the packaging and then put in a production order."

"I'm thrilled that you like it, Justin. I know what a tough customer you are."

"I don't like it, I *love* it. And I had an idea that might kill two birds with one stone: a second big launch party out in Los Angeles. We can put Parker in charge of it. It will get her out of our hair."

"That's a brilliant idea."

Avery hung up and walked back into Parker's room. She had switched on the television and was watching *The View*.

"I wish I could be on *The View*," Parker said.

Avery was tempted to remind her that the guests on *The View* had actually accomplished something.

"Parker, that was Justin. He sends you all his best wishes."

"He's a sweet guy. Smart, too," Parker said without taking her eyes off the television.

"He is smart—smart enough to think you should be in charge of the West Coast launch of the perfume."

It took it a moment to sink in, but then Parker muted the television and turned to Avery. "Really?"

"Yes, we want to have a big party out there and establish a presence very quickly. Both Justin and I think you're the perfect person to pull it all together. You're creative, you have great connections, and you know L.A. so well."

"Are you just doing this because you feel sorry for me?"

"Parker, you should know by now that when it comes to business, I don't play games."

Parker took this in and then said, "This is a big responsibility, isn't it?"

Avery nodded.

"And you and Justin really believe I can handle it?"

"We wouldn't have given it to you if we didn't."

Slowly, right in front of Avery's eyes, life and animation came back into Parker's face. "Oh my God, I have to get right to work. I know an amazing new club on Sunset that would be *perfect* for the party, and I can get every hot young actor and actress in town to come." She buzzed for a nurse. "Maybe it would be better to have it around a pool. The Roosevelt Hotel has gotten *très* hot. Wait—what about the Getty! Mom is on the board, I'm sure I could swing it!"

Avery felt relief flood over her. Parker would be out of her hair for the next couple of months. Plus, an L.A. launch party was a terrific idea. And she was giving Parker another chance, which was important because it honored Finn.

"Let's talk later and go over your ideas," Avery said.

The nurse appeared in the doorway.

"I need a pad and paper," Parker said to her.

The nurse made a disapproving *that's not my job* face, but said, "Okay" and disappeared.

Parker retrieved her makeup kit from the bedside table. She scrutinized her face in a hand mirror. "I look like shit," she said, and immediately started to apply foundation.

"Well, I better get back to the office," Avery said.

Without looking up from her makeup application, Parker said, "Oh, God, I know the feeling, I have *so much* work to do."

As she walked to the elevators, Avery had two thoughts. The first was, Justin is a genius. The second was, I *hate* Parker Adams.

25

PATRICIA LUCAS WAS living in a furnished sublet in Tudor City, a complex of ornate apartment buildings that were built in the 1920s and were located in the East Forties, near the United Nations. Avery had spoken to her a couple of times since their meeting at the Cloisters, but she couldn't shake her sense of betrayal and her feeling that Patricia had given her up for adoption because she was an impediment to her career. Avery remembered the way Patricia had told her the story of her birth that day, sitting on the ramparts, holding her head at a certain tilt to the sun, as if she knew it was her most flattering angle. It was a performance, and it only reinforced the contrast between her fame and success and Avery's struggle. Avery hadn't gotten to where she was by letting people play her for the fool. And while part of her wanted to be forgiving and build a relationship with Patricia, as she walked into the lobby of her building she was carrying a pretty heavy chip on her shoulder.

Patricia answered the door wearing an Annie Hall outfit of dark slacks, a white oxford shirt worn out, and a loose tie. "Darling," she said, giving Avery kisses on both cheeks and ushering her in.

The apartment was small and cramped, but Patricia had lit candles and placed flowers around, which helped disguise its flaws. Soft instrumental music was playing.

"Lucy called to say she'd be a little late, which is just as well. I wanted us to have some time alone," Patricia said. "Can I get you a glass of wine?"

"Sure," Avery said, sitting on a love seat. She looked around and noticed threadbare upholstery and a shelf of tiny porcelain shoes covered in a thick layer of dust.

Patricia poured them both glasses of white wine and brought over a tray of cheese and crackers. She sat beside Avery on the love seat. Avery wished Patricia had sat in one of the other chairs. She felt trapped and claustrophobic.

"I hear you had a successful trip to Europe," Patricia said.

Close up like this, even the forgiving candlelight couldn't hide the lines in Patricia's face or how much makeup she had on. Anxiety and unease flickered in the corners of her eyes.

"Yes, it went very well. I met with a master perfumer, a man who is a legend in the field." Avery wanted Patricia to know that she wasn't the only star in the room. For a moment, Avery considered telling Patricia about Brad. But no, they were a long way from girl talk.

"It's all so exciting," Patricia said. There was a pause. Patricia looked down into her wineglass and her face grew serious. "May I bring up something that's difficult for me to talk about?"

Avery took a long sip of her wine and didn't answer. After one perfunctory question about Avery, Patricia was turning the focus back on herself. Typical.

"As you well know, I've made some mistakes in my life," Patricia began. "Personal mistakes, career mistakes . . . financial mistakes." She exhaled with a sigh, nibbled on the edge of her lower lip. "After my Oscar nomination I was offered every movie in town, but I got on a high horse and passed on a lot of parts that I shouldn't have, holding out for the role of a lifetime. Well, that role never came." She took a cracker off the tray, spread cheese on it, and then put it back. "And I lost a lot of income while I waited. I've never had much of a head for money. I earned it, I spent it. Then I stopped earning, but I still kept spending." She laughed ruefully. "I did the big house thing. Boy, was that a mistake, but I thought I had to keep up appearances. Then there were the clothes, the fancy cars, the beauty treatments, the help. I woke up one day and it was all gone."

Avery found it hard to have a lot of sympathy for this tale of woe. Basically, Patricia blew it by getting too big for her britches. She finished off her glass of wine and quickly poured herself another. Her movements were abrupt, almost masculine, in sharp contrast to her usual grace and reserve. She took a long sip and her composure returned.

"So, about five years ago I sold the house, which was on its fourth mortgage, and moved to something much smaller, a bungalow really. I hustled for work, anything—guest shots, voice-overs. Word gets around. You know, Hollywood is terrified of a loser; it's like suddenly you have some deadly communicable disease. All the good work I'd done, all the terrific movies I had been in, no longer counted. I pretty much had to leave town to get a job. I did summer stock, dinner theater. But it was never enough. . . ." She finished off the wine and poured herself a third glass. "Oh, Christ, Avery, I'm going to stop beating around the bush. . . . I'm broke. Your mom is flat-on-her-ass broke. I mean, look at this place. . . ." She gestured to the cluttered room. "It looks like it was furnished at the Salvation Army. I rented it off craigslist."

Avery felt a mix of fascination and satisfaction, along with sympathy. She knew from firsthand experience how tough it was to be broke. Still, as someone who had struggled and sweated for everything she had, she found it hard to shed any tears for Patricia, who had easy early success and then threw it away by acting like a diva.

"I'm sure you'll find some work," Avery said.

Patricia stood up and walked to the window, looked out at the city. Without turning to Avery, she said, "Did you know that critics called me 'one of the major talents of her generation'? That's right, your mom was a contender. Every director in town wanted to work with me, the scripts poured in. Then there were the men; I had to fight off the suitors, every day roses would arrive, chocolate, jewelry . . . and I thought it would never end, that I would always be young and beautiful. . . ." Patricia let out a bitter little laugh. "Cue the violins . . . aging actress with a fondness for cheap wine takes a trip down maudlin lane. . . ."

Patricia turned from the window, sat in an armchair facing Avery.

"I need your help," she stated simply.

Avery was dumfounded by Patricia's performance, and it *was* a performance, leading up to the final beat—her urgent plea for help. What sort of help could she provide? She certainly wasn't in a financial position to cover Patricia's expenses, not on the salary she was paying herself at Flair. And was Avery supposed to feel pity for the tale of her fancy house, burning through money, fighting off suitors, all while Avery was fighting off her father and living on government cheese? Patricia wasn't her responsibility. Birth mother or not, she barely knew her. Still, it was cruel and sad to see how quickly Patricia dropped her cultured, winsome veneer, and the level of desperation that lurked behind it.

"I don't understand what you want from me," Avery said.

"Don't worry, I'm not asking you to take care of me. It's more of a hand up, not a handout," Patricia said, shifting into a more no-nonsense mode.

"What kind of a hand up?"

Patricia took a deep breath, leaned forward, and began. "Well, I've signed up with a manager here in New York. She's *good*, Avery, I mean she *believes* in me, in my talent. She specializes in reviving careers and she's helped me come up with a strategy to get mine moving. She says the key is to get my name and face out there again, refresh people's memories about Patricia Lucas, and introduce myself to a new generation. So . . . just to lay all my cards on the table here, the best way to do that would be to generate some human interest stories about *us*, you and me—our history, how I gave you up, then found you, your success. My manager is sure we can get a lot of media attention. The story is just a natural, it plays to so many issues—motherhood, redemption, healing." Patricia leaned back in her chair, crossed her legs, and sipped her wine, giving her proposal a moment to sink it.

Avery put down her wineglass. "Is that why you invited me to dinner? To pitch this idea of our inspiring little mother-daughter reunion filled with *redemption* and *healing*?" Patricia didn't say anything, which answered Avery's question. "I see. Well, Mom, didn't it cross your mind that I might feel completely used? Betrayed by you all over again? If I didn't have the potential to help you revive your career, would you have even gotten in touch with me?"

Again, Patricia said nothing.

"I'm serious, I want you to answer to that question. If I was just some housewife still living in Wilkes-Barre, would you have bothered? Or if I was sick, or in trouble of some kind? I bet you would have just left me alone to fend for myself, skipped the 'redemption' and 'healing.' But I can be useful, so you 'found' me, your long lost daughter who you love so very much."

"Avery, please don't judge me too quickly."

"I wish I'd judged you a little *more* quickly. It's all about *you*, isn't it? Don't you think it's time you started to think about *me*?" Avery stood up. "I'm going to leave now. Tell Lucy I'll see her in the office tomorrow."

Avery made for the door. Patricia was up in a flash and grabbed her wrist.

"You listen to me, young lady! Yes, it *is* all about me. *Okay?* Are you happy now, I admitted it? I'm almost fifty years old and I don't have a goddamn dime to my name! Do you have any concept of how terrifying that is? Well, *do you?*" Patricia's face was taut, her eyes narrow. "I'm standing at the edge of the abyss and it's a long way down and I will do *whatever* it takes to save myself. You think the world was handed to me on a platter? I've worked hard, goddamn hard, for everything I have. And let me tell you something else, do you think your drive and talent and beauty fell out of a tree? You got them from me—*your mother!*" Patricia let go of Avery's wrist and took a couple of deep breaths. When she spoke, her voice was low, but no less fervent. "Why don't you put on your thinking cap a minute? Publicity doesn't come easy in *any* business. We're *all* struggling. You want to make a splash with that perfume? I can help you. Imagine us booked on Oprah together, going on *The View*, on the cover of *People*. You think I'm the only one who would gain? Wake up, sweetheart, and smell the potential. Our story could do big things for one Avery Wilkins."

Avery stood there looking at Patricia, whose gaze was fierce and challenging.

Neither moved, neither spoke. The air was charged with electricity, hostility, and cunning.

The doorbell rang.

Patricia gave Avery a significant look. Then she ran her fingers through her hair, put a serene smile on her face, and went to answer the door.

"Mom!" Lucy cried, offering Patricia a big bouquet of flowers.

"Hello, darling girl," Patricia gushed, kissing her daughter on both cheeks.

"I'm afraid I'm going to have to eat and run. Karl wants me to meet him at a club. Oh, Mom, I have a beau, a real beau!" Lucy said. She walked into the room and hugged Avery. When she pulled back from the hug, she looked at Avery and asked, "Are you all right?"

There was a pause. Avery and Patricia looked at each other.

". . . Yes, I'm fine, just fine," Avery said. "It just threw me a little bit to see you both together. My birth mother and my sister."

"It's just us girls," Patricia said.

"The three mouseketeers," Lucy said.

"One for all, and all for one," Avery said, shooting Patricia a rueful, knowing glance.

26

THE MARKETING COMPANY that was running the focus group was in midtown. Avery and Justin were in a cab on their way there, and her anticipation grew more intense with each passing block. The only people who had smelled the perfume so far were Avery, Justin, and Brad. The focus group would be its unveiling. What if the young women in the group hated it, or thought it was dull, or old-fashioned? When it came to releasing a product, all the planning in the world didn't mean a thing if your customers didn't like it.

It was a bright warm day; summer was starting to take hold. Some people hated summer in the city. Not Avery. She loved the way the streets and cafés filled with people, and the casual clothes that everyone wore. But she loved it most of all because it brought back memories of her summer with Finn.

Almost as if he were psychic, Brad called on her cell.

"I'm back from Russia and I *really* want to see you."

"You do?"

"Yes, I have some news."

"Well, I'm on my way to the focus group."

"Give me the address, I'll meet you there."

"Brad, this is work."

"I understand, I'll meet you afterwards. I just want a few minutes of your time."

Avery hesitated. She and Brad hadn't seen each other since Paris. Although they'd talked a couple of times, their night at the Crillon hardly seemed real. Still, she missed him, missed his confidence, his energy, his conversation . . . and his touch. This heat made her feel . . . sensual.

"I'll call you when we're done," she said.

Janet Panken was the president of Marketing Strategies, Inc. Middle-aged and exuding a brisk confidence, she greeted Avery and Justin as they got off the elevator. She escorted them down a hallway.

"I think we've put together a very good group," she said. "We have eight working women from the ages of twenty-four to thirty-six, all of them regular perfume wearers and purchasers."

"Single? Married?" Avery asked.

"Two married, one engaged, five single."

Janet led them into a smallish room with low lighting. Through a one-way mirror they could see the focus group. The women were just settling in around a large oval table, helping themselves to juice, coffee, cookies. They were a diverse group racially, and all of them were attractive and pulled together. The room had hidden microphones and Avery could hear their casual banter. This was fun for them; they were on their lunch hours and were being paid a hundred dollars each.

"The woman at the end of the table is Lauren, our facilitator," Janet explained. "She'll be leading the discussion, coaxing out thoughts and opinions." There were two small bottles in front of Lauren, and glass vials holding dippers had been placed around the table.

"All right, ladies, we're just about to get started," Lauren said.

Avery leaned forward in her chair, barely able to contain her excitement. Just at that moment, a breathless Lucy appeared.

"I'm so sorry to interrupt, Avery, but this package arrived at the office from Henri Bihary in Paris and I thought it might be important so I cabbed uptown with it," Lucy said.

Avery felt a stab of annoyance. Couldn't the package have waited a couple of hours?

"We're just about to begin here," Avery said.

"I'm sorry, but since it was from Monsieur Bihary I thought you might want to have it before the focus group began," Lucy said. She was as sincere and eager as a puppy, and Avery was disarmed.

In the conference room, Lauren was saying, "All right, ladies, let's go around the table and introduce ourselves. Tell us your first name, your occupation, and your general thoughts on perfume."

Janet shot Avery a look that said *the train is leaving*.

Avery took the package from Lucy and quickly opened it. It contained a beautiful antique book entitled *Le Jardin d'Alchimie*. Avery quickly leafed through it. The book was filled with gorgeous illustrations of flowers and descriptions of their smells. It was a lovely sentiment, but it certainly could have waited.

In the conference room, the women were introducing themselves. Avery handed the book back to Lucy and whispered, "Would you take it back to the office with you, please."

Lucy nodded, but her eyes were riveted to the one-way mirror and she was hanging on every word the women were saying. The focus group was privileged information, but Lucy seemed so fascinated that Avery decided it would be okay for her to stay. She wanted a career in the business, so it was part of her education. Avery liked the idea of mentoring Lucy.

In the conference room, Lauren said, "Now I'm going to pass

around two small bottles of perfume. Please dip a blotter in the bottle, smell the perfume, and then give your initial impression. Just free-associate."

This was the moment Avery had been waiting for. She held her breath as the two small bottles were passed around.

"Oh, it's nice!" one young woman exclaimed. "Very nice."

"It smells so fresh and soft," another said.

Justin reached over and squeezed Avery's hand.

"It's like a summer afternoon, when you've been at the beach and then you take an outdoor shower and you just feel all relaxed and sensual."

"It's a little sharp at first."

"It's perfect for a date."

"I'd wear it, but probably not to a really formal party."

For the next forty-five minutes Avery was transfixed. The group discussed their reaction to the perfume and commented on the scent as it moved from top note to base. Finally Lauren asked the big question: would they buy it? Four of the women said that they definitely would, three said maybe, one said probably not.

"That is a *very* positive result," Justin said exultantly as the focus group broke up.

"It is indeed," Janet agreed.

Avery found herself obsessing on the negative reactions to the perfume. There was the woman who had found it too sharp, and another who wasn't sure she liked the woodsy aspect of the base note. And were the ones who said they loved it being truthful? The fact was the perfume could fail.

"There were some negatives in there," Avery said.

"Avery, there isn't a product on the planet that *everyone* likes," Justin assured her.

In spite of their reassurances, Avery felt a sudden stab of vulnerability, felt doubts burbling up from deep in her psyche. Somehow having Lucy there added to her insecurity. She was a reminder of Avery's bitter childhood, and of her feelings about Patricia and all the resentment she harbored about being abandoned. She didn't want her sister to know her truth or see her vulnerability. She heard echoes of her father's taunting, demeaning voice. Her secret shame was pulling her down, into a sea of self-doubt. She felt her sense of control slipping away.

"Excuse me, I have to use the ladies' room," she said.

Once she was in the privacy of the stall, she took out her cell phone and dialed Brad.

"How did it go?" he asked.

"Everyone says it went really well, but I'm not so sure it did."

"Avery, you sound frazzled."

"I'm lonely."

"Where are you?"

Avery gave him the address. He said he'd be there in fifteen minutes.

She hung up and opened the stall door. Lucy was standing there.

"Lucy, hi," Avery said, trying to contain her surprise. Had she followed Avery into the ladies' room? Had she been eavesdropping on her call with Brad?

"I hope you're not mad at me," Lucy said, a hangdog expression on her face.

"Mad at you?"

"For barging in at the last minute like that. I just thought that the package from Bihary might be helpful. I'm sorry."

"It's not a big deal, Lucy, but sometimes you're a little . . . well, overeager."

"I know I am, and I'm sorry. It's a fat girl thing. I overcompensate. And being with Karl has me a little dizzy. It's my first relationship, well, ever. And I guess I get a little nervous around you. Partly because you're my boss, of course, but also because you're my sister. I *admire* you so much, it's an honor to be working on your perfume . . . Oh, Lucy, shut up, you're gushing."

Once again, Avery was disarmed by Lucy's obvious sincerity and insecurity.

"Lucy, you're doing a terrific job at Flair. And I'm delighted that you've found a boyfriend. If I seem a little preoccupied at times, it's just because, well, I *am* preoccupied."

"Thank you for saying that," Lucy said. She rubbed her palms on her thighs, fidgeted, shrugged, and then she bounded over and hugged Avery.

It was an awkward hug, too tight, too tense, but it was heartfelt and Avery was touched. Avery yearned to open up to Lucy, to tell her the truth of her childhood, to share her pain and hurt with her sister. But she couldn't. The lockbox where she kept her secrets was buried too deeply.

"We should get moving," Avery said, gently pulling away from her sister's embrace.

As they rode down in the elevator, Justin said, "Lucy, I hope you understand that what you heard today is for your ears only."

"Of course."

When they were on the sidewalk outside the building, Avery said to Lucy, "We'll see you back at the office."

Lucy nodded and stood there for a moment. Both Avery and Justin looked at her, and she finally got the message. "See you soon," she said, and walked away.

"Avery, what's the matter?" Justin asked as soon as they were alone.

"Oh nothing."

"Don't oh-nothing me."

"Justin, do you *really* think the focus group went well?"

"I don't think it went well, I *know* it went well. Listen to me, Avery, what you're experiencing is a classic case of opening night jitters. Your baby is about to go out into the world and you're scared she won't be able to stand on her own two feet. Well, guess what? She can and she will. You—*you*, Avery Wilkins—have developed a fabulous perfume. We're going to settle on a name this afternoon, and then we'll meet with a packaging designer. There's no stopping us now."

Justin was so confident, so on top of everything. Why then did Avery still feel as if the ground was shifting beneath her?

"Thanks, Justin. Listen, I'll be back at the office in about an hour."

"Get yourself some lunch, your blood sugar is probably low," Justin said, giving her a kiss of reassurance before disappearing into the crowd.

27

NO SOONER WAS he gone than she saw Brad striding toward her. When he reached her, they stood looking at each other for a moment. His eyes were filled with kindness and strength.

"Avery," he said.

Then she was in his arms. They kissed and the emptiness inside her began to recede. She could breathe again. Everything would be all right.

"I've missed you," Avery whispered.

"Russia was agony. I couldn't get you out of my mind."

"Don't say that," she said, desperately wanting him to go on.

"But it's true. Come on," he said, taking her hand, leading them north.

"Where are we going?"

"You'll see."

As Brad led her briskly uptown, it felt like someone had spun the world around. Avery's mood went from dark to light. The day took on a sparkly, bubbly quality. Everywhere she looked she saw flowers and smiles. She was in Brad's hands and they were strong and secure.

They reached Central Park South. There was a line of horse-drawn carriages. Brad led her to the first one.

"We want to take a ride through the park," he told the driver, a middle-aged man with fat cheeks and droopy eyes.

"Yes, sir."

Brad bounded into the cab and then reached down and helped Avery up. He pulled up the roof and then sat down beside Avery on the seat. They were enclosed on three sides. He took a throw and spread it over their laps.

The driver gave the reins a shake and the horse turned into the park. It felt wonderfully cocooned inside the cab, their bodies in shadow.

"I know, I know, taking a hansom cab ride through Central Park is one of those silly clichéd things that only tourists do," Brad said, putting his arm around Avery.

"I didn't say that," Avery said.

"But I bet you were thinking it."

"I was thinking how nice it is to be this close to you. Please," she said, "tell me your news."

"I'm falling in love with you."

Avery knew, in that instant, as they passed a playing field, a game of softball, a spaniel racing across the grass, that her life would never be same again. She didn't know what to say, and wasn't sure she could speak in any case, so she just reached up and touched Brad's face.

They kissed again. As the carriage made its way slowly through the southern stretches of Central Park, they made out like a couple of teenagers. Except that when Avery was a teenager, she never had a boyfriend, was never kissed on a sunny afternoon. She had been running so hard for so long. Would she finally be able to stop?

"Oh, Brad," she moaned, "thank you for this."

She kissed him and felt a wild sense of freedom. Freedom from worry, from insecurity, from rage and pain and doubt. There was nothing but Brad, their bodies, their want . . . their love.

Avery lost track of time as they sprawled out on the seat in the shadows. There was something so exciting about being outside in the carriage, Brad straining against his clothes, she breathless, the sky dancing over their heads, his smell, his tongue, and then he placed his hand on her thigh and slid his fingertips up under her skirt *just a little but just enough* and a shudder coursed through her and then another and she bit her lip to stifle her cries and she collapsed against him, not knowing which she wanted more—to laugh or to cry.

28

AVERY ARRIVED BACK at Flair an hour later.

"Wow, do you look recharged, you are glowing!" Justin said as she swept into her office.

She plopped down in her desk chair, unable to contain a broad grin.

"If I didn't know better, I'd say you were in love," Justin said.

"Do you know better?"

"Oh-my-God, Brad is back."

"You gave me permission to skip in Paris. May I twirl in my office?"

"Once."

And so Avery stood up and did a joyful pirouette.

"Now that that's out of your system," Justin said with a smile, "we still don't have a name for the perfume. Oh, I took the liberty of calling Suzee Jones at *Stylish* magazine to tell her how fantastic it is. She wants you to go see her next Monday at 8 P.M. and to bring along a sample."

"That's fantastic news. But isn't 8 P.M. an odd time?"

"Avery, if she wanted to meet you underwater, you'd be there in a bikini."

"With my scuba gear."

"Amen. On another note, Parker just called."

"Oh God, she takes the twirl out of me every time. What's happening with her?"

Justin had rented Parker an office on Sunset Boulevard and hired her an assistant. She was going to AA and NA meetings every day, and seemed to be taking the West Coast launch very seriously.

"She claims that Johnny Depp is a definite for the L.A. launch party."

"That would be terrific, if it's true."

"But everything else is falling into place. Once we settle on the name and pick a couple of possible designs for the bottle, we can have prototypes within the week. Then we can take a little time deciding which packaging we like the best, and then it's into production. So nailing a name is crucial. *Now*."

"Let's do it," Avery said.

As if on cue, Lucy appeared in the doorway, holding a notebook.

"I hope I'm not interrupting?" she asked.

Lucy seemed to have radar that detected any important meeting. Avery knew how crucial timing was in business, and her sister seemed to have a real instinct. She felt a stab of sisterly pride.

"We're about to brainstorm for a name," Avery said.

"Oh-my-God, you're kidding. May I sit in? Please? I mean not if you don't want me to, but I'm just fascinated by the whole process." She took a step into the room and said in a more confident voice, "Maybe I could even be helpful."

"That's the right attitude. Sure, come on in," Avery said.

Lucy came in, sat, and got ready to take notes.

Justin called in several members of the senior creative staff, and when everyone was seated, he opened a folder and said, "All right, time to play the name game. . . ."

For the next two hours they batted around ideas. They thought that Radiance was strong, but not quite young enough; it brought to mind ball gowns and dinner dances. April Moon was a contender; it said spring, young, fresh, romance, but it was a bit old-fashioned sounding, like a song from the fifties. Everyone agreed that After the Rain was a great image of renewal and clean, fresh air, but you didn't get it right away; you had to think about it for a second.

They'd tossed around dozens of other names, gone through three pots of coffee, and frustration was starting to set it when Avery said, "What about Charm?"

Everyone sat in silence for a moment, and then Justin said quietly, "It's perfect."

Avery stood up and began to walk around the room, her voice rising in excitement. "It works on a couple of levels. A charm casts a spell, brings luck—in our case luck in love. And charm is a woman's indispensable asset. Plus it's short, sweet, effervescent, but definitely seductive."

"You could even put an actual charm on the bottle itself, like a crystal moon or something," Justin exulted. "We have our name!"

Avery did a little jig of joy, and laughter filled the room. Lucy dutifully took notes.

29

AVERY WAS ON her way to meet with Suzee Jones at the offices of *Stylish*. She had a sample of Charm with her. It was a balmy evening, and as she strode down the street, Avery felt strong and focused, her demons in check. Brad had been a rock. Unlike Marcus, he truly understood and accepted the demands of her career. Probably because he was so driven himself. In fact, he'd been out in Chicago on business all week. They spoke every night, long relaxed getting-to-know-each-other talks about their respective days, about their taste in books and TV shows and food, about their future. Avery would sit in bed as they talked, propped up on pillows and suffused with a feeling of comfort and security she hadn't known since Finn's death.

Stylish was headquartered in a sleek tower just off Times Square. The building was quiet at this hour, with all the nine-to-fivers long gone. As the elevator whisked her up to the thirty-seventh floor, her adrenaline rose with it. Being featured in *Stylish* would catapult Flair, and Avery, to the next level. Avery had an instinctive feeling that modesty would go over well with Suzee

Jones. She was so hard-charging herself, Avery thought competing on that level would be a mistake. It would be shrewder to play the humble supplicant, here to render unto Suzee.

The elevator opened to a large open space with curving walls, glass brick, and geometric furniture. The walls showcased blowups of *Stylish* covers. The place was empty.

Then Suzee appeared, wearing a belted robe over a spandex leotard. "Hello there," she said with a big smile. "I was just finishing up my yoga when Reese called—and you don't put Reese on hold. She has a new house and we're mad crazy to get it into the magazine. It's so great to see you. Come on back."

Avery followed her through the open space and into her large private office. In contrast to the rest of the place, it was casual, even a little messy. A desk faced a couple of comfy couches and bookcases filled with pictures of her husband and children.

"My life is perfectly organized chaos," Suzee said with a bright laugh. "Three kids, two houses, two dogs, one job, one husband—and one helluva stress level. But you know all about that, Miss Founder and CEO."

"I sure do."

"You look as a cool a cuke," Suzee said.

"It's all an illusion."

"Illusion is its own reality," Suzee said, and they laughed. "Thanks for coming in at this hour, it's so hectic during the day. I wanted to give you my full attention."

"It's my pleasure."

"Sit, relax. Let's talk a minute."

Avery sat on one of the couches. Suzee went to a small bar. "Now that I've done my yoga it's time for my reward: a lemondrop. I hope you'll join me."

"I'd love one."

"I think of it as a vitamin infusion—C is so good for the skin."

Suzee deftly mixed a small pitcher of chilled lemon vodka, lemon juice, and sugar syrup. She poured the drinks into two martini glasses and joined Avery on the couch.

"Cheers," she said, raising her glass.

They clinked and sipped. The drink was tart and sweet—and potent.

"This is delicious," Avery said, feeling herself relax.

"I live for my daily lemondrop. That's off the record, of course. On the record I live for my husband and kids."

They laughed again.

"So your perfume is ready to meet the world."

"I hope."

"Ah, modesty—always refreshing," Suzee said.

"You must know that little tug of insecurity right before you roll something out," Avery said.

"Little tug? How about a swirling vortex?"

"But you've done so well," Avery said.

"Thanks. I know my market . . . and I work like a dog. So let's see what you've got."

Avery took the bottle of Charm out of her bag. Suzee opened the bottle and dabbed some on her wrists and behind her ears. "Oh, it's delicious!"

"Thank you," Avery said.

"Terrific top notes—fresh, bright." Suzee brought her wrist up to her nose. "Oh, here come the heart notes . . . so sensual, a floating bed of blossoms." She closed her eyes and waited a moment. "Now the base is coming into focus . . . white cedar . . . earthy, full, a little erotic." She opened her eyes, looked at Avery, and said, "I love it! It's young and fun, sexy but not sleazy. It's perfect for Stylish. Our readers will adore it."

Avery felt a surge of triumph course up her spine.

"And you're a real role model. You founded a successful company while still in your twenties, and now you're topping it all off with this sensational perfume. This deserves a little refresher," Suzee said. As she went and got the pitcher from the bar, Avery couldn't help feeling like she was the one being flattered. Odd.

Suzee sat back down and topped off both their glasses. She raised hers and said, "To Charm."

"To Charm," Avery said.

They clinked again. Avery took a sip and enjoyed the euphoric warmth that spread through her body.

"I see a big fat feature in *Stylish*. I'm going to make a prediction: Avery Wilkins is going be famous by this time next year."

"I can't tell you how much I appreciate this."

"There's nothing I like more than helping young talent," Suzee said. Then she leaned back on the sofa and crossed her legs. "There is one thing you can do for me."

"Name it," Avery said.

Suzee reached for a leather portfolio on the table and handed it to Avery. She opened it—it was filled with modeling photos of a pretty girl who looked to be about seventeen or eighteen. Many of the pictures had the model's name on the bottom: Aimee Jones.

"That's my daughter," Suzee said with maternal pride. "She just did a six-page layout for next month's *Glamour*. Doesn't she have a wonderful look?"

"She's very pretty," Avery said.

"Of course, I'm wildly biased, but I think she's going to be a supermodel. You know what would be the best thing for her right now?"

"What?"

"To be picked as the face of Charm. She's perfect—young and fresh and full of energy," Suzee said.

"She should definitely come to our audition," Avery said in measured tones.

There was a pause, and the comfort level between the two women plummeted. Suzee ran her fingers through her hair. "I actually think just announcing that Aimee Jones has been picked would be a much stronger move."

"That's not going to happen," Avery said, suddenly feeling quite sober.

Suzee took this in for a long moment, and when she spoke her voice was dry and had an edge. "Do you realize what a feature in *Stylish* would mean for Charm, and for you?"

"I think so, yes," Avery said.

"I'm not quite sure you do. We reach six million young women. That's a lot of perfume. I could change your life. Aimee is ideal for Charm. I'm not asking you to do anything untoward."

"You're asking me to compromise my professional standards. Aimee looks like a very pretty girl, but if you think I'm going to make her the face of Charm on the basis of a quick look at her book, you're wrong."

The two women looked at each other for a long tense moment.

"Be very careful here," Suzee said finally.

"No, you be careful. I don't know who you think you're dealing with, but I don't stand for being played like that. I'm going to find the best model for my perfume and I'm going to do it my way."

"I'd hate to see you lose that feature," Suzee said.

"I'd rather lose the feature than lose my integrity."

"I think you're very naïve," Suzee said.

"And I think you're very cynical." Avery stood up, put the bottle of Charm back in her purse, and said, "You might want to finish off that cocktail. It will make it easier for you to live with yourself."

Then she turned and walked out of the office.

30

IT WAS THE next morning, and Avery and Justin were in a huddle in her office. She had just told him the story of her visit with Suzee Jones.

"You handled it perfectly," he said in admiration. "It's a shame to lose the feature, but if you get a reputation as being for sale, it will kill us in the long run."

"And maybe we won't lose the feature."

"What do you mean?"

"What goes around comes around."

"Sounds like you've got something up your sleeve."

"Let's just say I'll keep my eyes open for an opportunity," Avery said with a sly smile.

"I do have to give Suzee some credit for her timing, because the next big item on our agenda is the casting of the model who actually is going to be the face of Charm," Justin said.

"It's so important to find just the right girl. She has to be classy but not snooty, and beautiful but in a friendly, approachable way," Avery said.

"I think we should turn the casting session into a media event," Justin said. "We'll hold it at Marc Tanner's studio, shoot a video, get all the entertainment shows to cover it, do a live podcast on flair .com. Could be a publicity bonanza."

"You're brilliant," Avery said.

"Aw shucks, 'tain't nuthin'," Justin said with a big grin. "Let me go get this ball rolling."

Justin left and Avery was alone at her desk. Her thoughts turned to Brad. He had told her that he loved her. But she had learned to guard her heart closely. Finn had been the first man she had let in, and he had been killed. Then Marcus, and he had betrayed her. Could she really trust Brad with her most precious possession? The thought of him filled her with longing, but was she ready to make herself vulnerable, to love again with all her heart?

Her phone rang, pulling her from her reverie.

"Darling, it's your mom."

"Hi, Patricia."

"I have the most marvelous news."

"Yes?"

"*People* wants to do a story on us, on our reunion. Isn't that thrilling?" Patricia said.

"It could certainly be good publicity," Avery admitted.

"Oh, it could make all the difference for me. And with *People* on-board, we can go to Barbara Walters. Maybe even Oprah. The story is a natural for her. My manager says it's all about parlaying one thing into another."

"Does she?" Avery said.

"You don't sound too enthusiastic."

"I'm going along with this little sham called our relationship for one reason: because it's in my best interests. Don't expect me to show a lot of phony enthusiasm when it's just the two of us."

There was a pause and then Patricia said cheerily, "I've moved to a new apartment."

"That was fast."

"It's another furnished sublet, but much nicer. I couldn't have photographers and television crews coming into that dump. It's all about appearances, sadly. What's *inside* seems to matter less and less these days. But what's inside my heart is enormous gratitude that you're in my life. As time goes on, you'll see. Your mother is a woman of substance."

"So what's the next step?"

"Can you come for tea on Wednesday? *People* will be here to take pictures and interview us both."

"I'll be there."

"They're coming at four, so why don't you come at three?" Patricia said. "We can chat a bit, get a sense of lighting and placement. And we can go over our stories, to make sure they're in sync."

"If we tell the truth about what happened, they'll be in sync."

"Of course, darling. That's what I meant."

"Okay, Patricia, I'll see you then."

Avery hung up. Patricia was trying to manipulate her like she was a marionette. Well, two could play that game.

Lucy appeared in her doorway, beaming. "May I come in?"

"Sure."

"Justin asked me to help him with the casting session buzz," she said, bounding over to Avery's desk. "So I got on the phone and called E! They want to send a video crew, if we give them an exclusive."

"Boy, that was fast." Lucy was really proving herself to be capable, aggressive, and sharp. And unlike with her scheming mother, there were no hidden agendas. "Thanks for the great work on this, and in general. Everyone is raving about you."

Lucy flushed and looked down at her hands. "Thank you for giving me this chance. I love working here. When I have a challenge, I just ask myself: WWAD? What Would Avery Do?" She looked up and smiled, her eyes glistening. "Having you for my big sister feels like one of the most important things that's ever happened to me. I feel less alone. I know we'll always be there for each other."

Avery felt her throat tighten. "I feel the same way," she said, feeling protective of Lucy.

"Now I have someone to talk to about Mom, someone who really understands."

"Patricia just called," Avery said.

Lucy grimaced slightly. "Is she coming on too strong for you?"

"She's very determined," Avery said.

"I try and detach from her. It's the only way I can protect myself emotionally."

"What was it like being raised by her?"

"In a word: erratic. She careened from overkill, you know, obsessive smother-love, to gee-Mom-I-haven't-heard-from-you-in-six-months. My dad did most of the grunt work," Lucy said.

"She's very manipulative," Avery said.

"It's too bad they don't give out Oscars for best emotional blackmail."

"I can't shake this suspicion that she only tracked me down because I can be useful to her."

"Sometimes I feel like I'm just a bit player in *The Patricia Lucas Story*. I remember one year when I was about ten, we spent months planning a Christmas trip to Catalina. We rented a suite at the Avalon. We were going to go horseback riding, boating, shopping, just the two of us. Then two days before Christmas she got a call inviting her to fly down to Acapulco, there was some big party. Guess which she chose?" Lucy said.

"I'm sorry, Lucy, that must have been so painful."

"I was devastated. I didn't get out of bed for four days. After that I just stopped expecting anything from her. I also put on thirty pounds."

"Well, you've recovered very well," Avery said. "And there's always the gym."

Lucy's cell phone rang, she checked the number. "It's Karl, I won't answer it."

"You can if you want."

"No, it's unprofessional."

"So things are still going well between you two?"

"So well I can hardly believe it. He's adorable, smart, funny, and lives on a pedestal. Seriously, he's wonderful. Best of all, he likes me."

"And what does he do?"

"He's in information services, but please don't ask me exactly what that means. But he must do well, he's got a great apartment."

"I'm happy for you, sis."

Lucy mock-slapped herself on the cheek. "Okay, back to business. I'm going to find the city's hippest caterer for the casting session."

"I'm sure you will." Avery's phone rang. She checked the incoming number: Brad. "Sorry, boss's prerogative," she said to Lucy before answering the call. "Hi, there. Are you back in town?"

"I am. And I've got two tickets to a Natural Resources Defense Council benefit at Roseland tonight. Sting is going to perform. Does it interest you at all?"

Avery ran a hand up the back of her neck and lowered her voice. "If you'll be there."

"Why don't you come by my place at seven, you haven't seen it yet. I promise all my dirty socks will be out of sight."

"That's disappointing. I want to see the real Brad."

"Oh, you will."

"Can't wait. . . . Here's another call coming in. . . . Oh, damn, it's Parker, I better take it. See you this evening. . . . Hi, Parker."

"I booked the Griffith Observatory for the launch party! It's so hip, so gorgeous, we're going to have the party of the year."

"Good work."

There was a pause. "Avery, thank you for trusting me with this," Parker said. "I've been going to my meetings."

"I'm proud of you."

"I love you, Avery."

Avery couldn't bring herself to return the sentiment. "Keep me posted on every update. And thanks again for the great work." Avery hung up and said to Lucy, "So, do you want to call E! and tell them it's a go?"

"Of course."

"I'm going out with Brad tonight . . . and I think I'll wear Charm," Avery said with a grin.

"You always wear charm," Lucy said with one of her big puppy-dog smiles.

31

BRAD LIVED IN a stately prewar building that was one of the best addresses on Central Park West. A uniformed doorman opened the door for Avery, a second nodded as she crossed the lobby, and a third manned the elevator that whisked her up to the twelfth floor. She stepped off the elevator to find Brad standing in the open doorway of his apartment.

"You look sensational" were the first words out of his mouth.

Avery had only had twenty minutes to get ready, so she went with a little black dress, black high-heel sandals, and silver earrings and bracelet.

"And you smell even better," Brad said as she got closer.

And then they were kissing. His body was strong and charged with want. Being out in the hallway added an erotic thrill. What if a neighbor appeared? Avery leaned into him, matching his want with her own.

"Would you like to step inside?" Brad said.

"I thought you'd never ask."

A large entry gave way to expansive living and dining rooms. It was an extravagance of open space accentuated by uncluttered modern décor. The clean cool lines were softened by cozy seating and warm lighting.

"This is incredible," Avery said.

"All the credit goes to my decorator," Brad said. "If it was left to me, it would be a wide-screen TV and a couple of couches. And the dirty socks, of course."

"And look at the view," Avery said, crossing to the window. Below them, Central Park spread out in the gathering twilight. The trees were topped by a sea of soft green leaves, lit by the glow of street lamps.

"I never get tired of it," Brad said, coming up behind her and wrapping his arms around her waist.

Avery leaned back against him and they stood there together. Their bodies felt so right, so solid, they just fit. Lovely light jazz was pouring from hidden speakers. The music was soulful, sexy, and buoyant. Avery melted into it.

"Would you like to see the rest of the place?" Brad asked in a whisper.

"I want to see it all," Avery whispered back.

He took her hand and led her to the kitchen.

It was large, modern, and from what she could tell, unused.

"This is the kitchen," Brad said.

"It's a nice kitchen."

He led her into the library. "This is the library," he said, his arm around her waist.

"It's a nice library."

She ran her fingertips lightly down his arm and across the top of his hand. She brought his hand up to her mouth and kissed it. He made a little moaning sound.

"There's a guest bedroom, and then the master," he said, "which would you like to see first?"

"Whichever is closest."

32

THE NRDC BENEFIT was a hot ticket. Roseland was packed with hundreds of young people
in full party mode, dancing, drinking, and flirting. A rumor that
Leonardo DiCaprio was going to show up ratcheted the energy
level even higher.

Avery and Brad were out on the dance floor, surrounded by
writhing bodies. They were grinning at each other, riding the wave
of the music, the crowd, and their mutual magnetism.

Then Avery saw Marcus.

He was making his way toward them through the mass of dancing bodies, a determined expression on his face.

"Hi, babe," he shouted over the music. It was clear he'd been
drinking and was loaded for bear. "And you must be the famous
Brad."

Avery stopped dancing, and sighed with a mixture of exaspera-
tion and dread. She wasn't about to stand in the middle of this hul-
labaloo and shout. She took Brad's hand and led him off the dance

floor. Marcus followed. They made it to the relative quiet of the lobby. Marcus was sweating and looked a little wild-eyed.

"Brad Henry, this is Marcus Roland," Avery said.

Brad stuck out his hand. "Nice to meet you."

"I wish I could say the same, my friend," Marcus said, ignoring the handshake. "But I don't like guys who are going to hurt Avery."

"Marcus, I think you've had a little too much to drink," Avery said.

"I think you're going to want to have way too much to drink after I tell you about your buddy Brad here," Marcus said.

A concerned look flashed across Brad's face. "Listen, Marcus, why I don't I get you a cup of coffee."

"I don't want a fucking cup of coffee, I want to talk to my friend Avery."

"She may not want to talk to you right now," Brad said.

"I think we should let Avery be the judge of that." Marcus turned to her, his face filled with the wounded rage of a male ego that's taken a hard hit. "Well, Avery, do you want to hear what I have to say or not? . . . Before you answer, I think you should know that it concerns little Brad here and it ain't pretty. You might say I've been doing a little bit of opposition research."

Brad moved close to Marcus. "I don't have to stand here and listen to this."

Marcus stuck out his chest until the two men were face-to-face. "Feel free to leave. Avery deserves better than you anyway."

"A drunken wannabe like you, maybe?"

"I may have had a couple of drinks tonight, and I may not be as rich as you, but at least I'm not a murderer."

Brad slugged Marcus. Hard. He went down.

Sprawled out on the floor, Marcus looked up at them, his face twisted into an acid grin, blood trickling from the corner of his mouth. "Guess I struck a nerve."

"Come on, Avery, let's get out of here," Brad said.

"Oh, it's a hit-and-run," Marcus said, getting to his feet.

"Brad, what is he talking about?" Avery asked.

Brad let out a deep sigh. "I was going to tell you myself. . . ."

"Tell me what?"

There was a long pause.

"He killed his wife," Marcus said in a surprisingly calm voice.

Avery looked from one man to the other. "I don't understand."

"Avery, it's much more complicated than that, we need to talk . . . ," Brad began.

"He stabbed her with a kitchen knife, right in the heart," Marcus said.

Avery just stood stock still, trying to absorb the words. Then she turned to Brad. "Is that true?"

Brad put a hand on her shoulder. "I can explain everything. . . ."

Avery stepped away from him. "I asked you if it was true."

Brad looked her right in the eye . . . and nodded.

33

AVERY STOOD THERE in shock. She felt like she'd been punched in the stomach. The air was knocked out of her. Then a terrible hurt swept over her. She felt dizzy and there was ringing in her ears. She needed air, fresh air. She turned and rushed out of the club. Brad followed.

"Wait!" Brad called.

She turned and looked at him. He looked resolute, as if there was actually some way he could explain what he had done. Avery couldn't believe that just a few hours earlier they had been in bed together, making passionate love. It was happening all over again, just like it had with Finn and then Marcus. She suddenly felt like she was drowning, suffocating under a sea of pain and lies. She gasped for air.

"Aren't you going to let me explain?" he said.

"Explain!? Explain murder?"

"It wasn't murder, Avery. It was self-defense." He was fervent; his eyes were burning. Was it truth she saw in them? Or more lies? She couldn't tell anymore. And she certainly couldn't trust. "I'll tell you the whole story, if you just give me the chance."

"Don't you think you should have told me a long time ago?"

"No," he said simply. "I was very attracted to you and I wanted to see more of you, and if I'd told you it might have scared you off. When I want something I go for it. I wanted you. I *want* you."

He looked right into her eyes, no apology.

"Please. Let's go somewhere quiet, get a drink, and talk. I can explain everything. If, when I'm done, you want to leave, I won't try to stop you," Brad said.

Looking into his eyes, Avery felt an undertow, pulling her toward him against her will.

"We can't run away from this," Brad said. "I owe you an explanation and you owe me the chance to give it."

Avery hesitated, took a deep breath . . . and said, "All right."

34

THEY WERE SITTING at a back table in a homey restaurant popular with the theater crowd; it had exposed brick walls, show posters, a long wooden bar. Avery was drinking a vodka and tonic, Brad a scotch and water.

"My wife, Alexandra, was unstable. I knew she was high-strung when I married her, but she was also bright and a lot of fun. She never told me that she'd had a psychotic break as a teenager and been institutionalized. That she was a diagnosed manic depressive," Brad said.

Avery was listening to Brad, but she kept hearing Marcus's words: *He stabbed her with a kitchen knife.* She felt numb inside, unable to feel any more pain, as if her heart had been anesthetized.

"Over the years of our marriage, she became more and more erratic. She was medicated on a mix of antidepressants and antianxiety pills, and was drinking heavily. Then she became very paranoid. The more I tried to get her help, the more she thought I was part of some conspiracy to have her locked up forever."

"Why didn't you move out?" Avery asked.

"Because I felt responsible for her. Her psychiatrist told me that if I left there was a good chance she'd kill herself."

"So you did it for her," Avery said.

"That's completely unfair."

"It may be, but I'm angry at you. I should have heard this story that first night we went out. You're a murderer. I had a right to know that."

"For Christ's sake, Avery, I am not a murderer. I was charged with manslaughter. Two days later, the charges were dropped. It was self-defense. I came home one night and she came at me with the knife. She was hysterical, completely out of control, in the middle of a psychotic fit. I was protecting myself, we struggled, and the next thing I knew the knife was in her chest. If I hadn't fought her off, I'd be dead."

Brad put a hand on Avery's. She withdrew hers.

"Even if everything you're saying is true, you should have told me."

"I was about to. You have to believe me."

"Your credibility is pretty low."

"You're being awfully hard on me. We both know that something big and wonderful is happening between us."

"*Was* happening between us."

"Are you saying it's over?"

"I'm saying you're not the man I thought you were," Avery said.

"Look, I know you're in shock and I don't blame you for being skeptical."

"Your first marriage failed, your second ended in . . . this. What would *you* think?"

Brad polished off his drink and ordered another. "That's a fair question. I think I'd try to avoid snap judgments. I'd look at the facts of what happened. You can Google my wife's death. There were articles in the Seattle paper. Read about it. I've been working very hard to put it behind me. Alexandra was going to kill me. I wasn't about to let that happen."

Avery felt a grudging respect for his matter-of-fact honesty, his refusal to sugarcoat the pill. He ran his fingertip along the rim of his glass. He looked so serious in the pale light of the restaurant.

"I think we're a good match, Avery," he said. "I've never felt this strongly about anyone before, ever."

"I have strong feelings for you, too, Brad. I think you know that. But I'm going to need some time to sort out how I feel about all this." Avery stood up. "I'll be in touch when I'm ready."

Brad stood, too. "Just like that, you're leaving?"

"Yes."

"Can I walk you out and get you a cab?"

"I'd rather you didn't."

"Avery, I'm sorry I didn't tell you earlier."

"So am I."

They looked at each other across a sea of longing.

"Are you saying that we're over?"

"We're certainly over for tonight," Avery said.

35

AVERY WALKED OUT into the night. The jingle-jangle lights and sounds of the theater district swirled around her. She was restless and her muscles were twitching, she was uncomfortable in her skin. She wished she could be somewhere else, be someone else. If she went home, she would spend hours pacing her tiny apartment, running the events of the night over and over in her head.

There was only one way out: work. Since she was a little girl, work had been her refuge and her solace. When she was working the pain melted away; she was strong, right where she was supposed to be. She decided to walk down to the office. The exercise would burn off some of her tension.

The office building was eerily quiet at this hour. Avery stepped off the elevator, walked through the reception area and into the darkened main space. Across the way she noticed something strange.

There was light filtering out from under the closed door to her office.

Was someone in there?

She stopped and listened. She heard muffled voices. She walked stealthily, silently across the floor. When she got close to the door, she stopped and cocked her ear. She heard whispers:

"Hurry up!" It was Lucy's voice.

"Relax, will you," a male voice answered.

Avery stepped forward and opened the door. Lucy was watching anxiously as a man took pictures of papers that lay on her desktop.

"I hope I'm not interrupting," Avery said.

Lucy let out a yelp, and the man muttered, "Shit."

"You haven't answered my question."

There was a long tense pause before Lucy spoke. "Um, Avery, this is Karl Bover. Karl, this is my sister, Avery Wilkins."

Karl was about thirty and looked like Humpty Dumpty's conniving cousin. He was chubby and bald, with a smug baby face and shifty eyes behind rimless glasses. He stood up straight and jutted out his weak chin. "Hi, Avery, what a pleasure to meet you," he said, giving her an oily smile. "Lucy was just showing me around the office."

"See anything interesting?"

"Photography is a hobby of mine. That and quail hunting."

"They can both be risky," Avery said. She walked over to him and took the digital camera out of his hand. The document he'd been photographing was the formula for Charm. She calmly put it back in its folder and put the folder back in the drawer. Then she deleted the pictures from the camera. "Now, Karl, it's time for you to tell me who you're working for."

He didn't answer.

"You have ten seconds to tell me before I call the police—and you've already used up five," Avery said, taking out her cell phone.

"Aquavage," Karl said as sweat broke out on his upper lip.

Aquavage was a French cosmetics giant making a big push in the American market. A direct competitor to Flair.

"Interesting," Avery said. "Aquavage has a lot of money. They're going to need it. Tell your bosses that I'll be touch regarding a settlement."

Karl nodded numbly. Avery was silent for a few moments; she just stood there and enjoyed the sight of this scheming creep twisting in the wind.

"I assume you can find your own way out?" she said finally.

He nodded again.

Lucy was quivering, trying to hold herself together. "Should I go with him?" she asked.

"No, Lucy, I think you and I need to have a little chat."

Karl skulked out of the room. Lucy stood there with her head down, unable to meet her sister's gaze. Avery looked at her for a long moment, trying to absorb her betrayal.

"Well, Lucy," she said finally, "I think we just found out what kind of *information services* your beau provides."

Lucy's eyes grew wide with fear and she started to cry. "I'm sorry, Avery, I'm so sorry."

"One question: did you tell him you worked for me when you first met him?"

Lucy bit her lower lip and nodded. It was so pathetic. Karl was a slimy operator who took advantage of a desperately insecure, overweight girl to earn himself a serious paycheck.

"Everything you learned about Flair went right to Karl, didn't it?"

"He told me he was just really curious about the business."

"Okay, you've officially been had."

"Don't say that, please don't say that, *he loves me*," Lucy sobbed. "You don't understand, Avery, because you're *beautiful*. I'm not even pretty and I'm *fat*. Nobody wants a fat girl. I've never had a boyfriend before and Karl loves me, Avery, *he loves me*."

"I don't think he loves you, Lucy, I think he's just been using you. And even if he did love you, so what? He's a total sleazebag."

"How can you say that, how can you be so mean?" Lucy wailed.

"Since the day we met, I have given you nothing but unconditional friendship, support, and encouragement. Not to mention a job. And you call me mean?"

"I'm sorry, but he made love to me, he made me feel like a woman. He took me out to dinner and bought me flowers, he was a gentleman."

"I think you're very naïve, Lucy. This is a tough lesson, but one you need to learn."

Lucy turned on her with blazing eyes and hissed, "You're so hard!"

"Life is hard, Lucy," Avery said evenly. "I'm not interested in living in the land of delusions."

Avery took a box of tissues out of a drawer and handed them to Lucy. She wiped at her face, choked down her sobs, tried to pull herself together.

"You know I can't have you working here anymore, don't you?"

Lucy nodded.

"Pack up your desk and leave now."

"Do I have to do it now?"

"Yes."

"But we're sisters."

"Whatever that means."

36

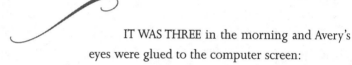

IT WAS THREE in the morning and Avery's eyes were glued to the computer screen:

CHARGES DROPPED IN HIGH-PROFILE CASE

King County District Attorney Allen Davis today dropped manslaughter charges against prominent Seattle businessman Brad Henry in the stabbing death of his wife, Alexandra Henry. Davis released the following statement: "After examining the forensic and circumstantial evidence, it was clear that this was either an accidental death or a suicide. When Mr. Henry arrived home at 10:30 P.M. on the night of April 12, his wife attacked him with a 12-inch kitchen knife. Mr. Henry sought to defend himself. In the ensuing struggle, the knife entered Ms. Henry's chest and punctured her heart." The District Attorney also released Ms. Henry's toxicology report. Her blood alcohol level was .20, indicative of severe alcohol poisoning. In addition, Demerol, Vicodin, and Xanax were found in her blood. Ms. Henry's psychiatrist, Dr. Gary Somers, released the following statement: "Ms. Henry was suffering from manic depression and acute paranoid psychosis. She was a danger to herself and others, but fought my attempts to have her institutionalized. During the three years that she was under my care, Mr. Henry made every possible effort to help and support his wife. This is a tragedy for all involved." Attempts to reach Mr. Henry for comment were unsuccessful. He remains in seclusion at his Seattle home.

Avery turned off her computer and sat there. She was in some realm beyond exhaustion. Thoughts ricocheted around in her head like an out-of-control pinball machine. So Brad had been telling the truth. Hadn't he? Would she ever know what really happened that night? If he had nothing to hide, why did he hide it from her?

Avery looked over at her bed. It looked like it was a thousand miles away. Her body felt like all the blood had been drained out of it, and it could just melt into nothingness. But she needed to sleep. She folded her arms on her desk and rested her head.

She fell asleep, but in her dreams she saw that knife.

37

AVERY WALKED ACROSS the lobby of the Hilton, on her way to a luncheon celebrating the American Women in Media Awards. No matter what was happening with Brad, Lucy, Parker, and Patricia, she wasn't about to drop the ball on Flair and the perfume. A lot of the top women executives in television, magazines, and the web would be at the lunch, and Avery was there to network. With Charm coming out in a matter of months, now was the time to get out there and talk it up.

Avery's anger at Lucy was turning into pity. She was still just a kid, desperately insecure and longing for romance. Enter Karl Bover, just the type of scheming creep who takes advantage of needy girls like Lucy. Yes, Lucy had betrayed her, but it was an unthinking betrayal by a naïve and impressionable young woman whose head was turned by the attentions of a sleazy manipulator. And there was one other thing about Lucy that Avery couldn't forget: she *was* her sister. And that meant something. Avery felt a blood connection to her, deep in her bones. In many ways, Lucy was as alone in the world as she was. Their relationship was important to both of them. It was worth fighting for.

As for Brad, Avery just couldn't shake her nagging misgivings. Images of what had happened the night that his wife died haunted her. Couldn't he have knocked the knife out of her hand? Surely he was much stronger than she was? Should she confront him with her doubts? Could she ever completely trust him?

As she approached the door to the ballroom, Avery stood tall, took a few deep breaths, and focused her attention on the task at hand. She reached the check-in table. A poster on a nearby easel showcased the women being honored. There was Suzee Jones, winner in the Best Women's Magazine category. Avery had known Suzee was one of the honorees, but she wasn't going to let that keep her from attending. In fact, she hoped they crossed paths.

"Avery Wilkins, from Flair Cosmetics," she said to the eager young woman manning the reception table.

"Oh, I love your products. Your blush is amazing. I'm wearing it now."

"You look terrific."

"Thanks to you," the girl said.

Avery felt a surge of pride. It was moments like this that made it all worth it.

The young woman handed Avery an identification badge and she walked into the ballroom. It was filled with hundreds of well-dressed women who exuded power and ambition. There were also a fair number of men. The program hadn't started yet, and things were still at the mix-and-mingle stage.

"Hi, Avery."

Avery turned—there was Marcus.

They looked at each other. The spark was still there. Marcus looked clear-eyed and sober.

"Marcus, hi. I wasn't expecting to see you here."

"*Timeline* is doing a segment on the most powerful women in the industry. We're here to get some footage," he said, indicating two cameramen who were roving the ballroom.

There was a pause and Avery tried to resist the attraction she was feeling. The last thing she needed was another complication to her romantic life.

"I've started therapy, Avery," Marcus said.

"That's admirable."

"It's also long overdue."

"How is it?"

"Painful. He has me talking about stuff I don't even like to think about," he said. "We've already figured out that I have problems with commitment, anger, and impulse control."

There was something irresistible about his sincerity. He was like a kid finally taking responsibility for his actions.

"I'm impressed."

"And I'm not doing it just to try and win you back," he said with a little grin. Suddenly he wasn't so sincere—which made him even more irresistible.

"I'll pretend I didn't hear that, but you and your therapist should definitely discuss the fact that you said it."

There was another pause.

"You look beautiful, Avery," Marcus said, lowering his voice.

"Okay, Marcus, let's nip this in the bud. I'm here to work." Then she spotted Suzee Jones across the room.

Avery had a brainstorm that made her pulse quicken.

She leaned into Marcus and hurriedly filled him in on her scheme.

"Are you in?" she asked.

"Of course," he said.

They headed across the ballroom to Suzee. Avery noticed women eyeing Marcus. Some of them were practically salivating. It was exciting to be with the sexiest man in the room, one of the sexiest men in the city.

When she saw Avery, a look of unpleasant surprise flashed across Suzee's face, but she quickly recovered with a big smile.

"Suzee Jones, I'm Marcus Roland, producer from *Timeline*."

"*What* a pleasure," Suzee said, shaking his hand.

"And you know Avery Wilkins," Marcus said, putting his arm around Avery's waist and pulling her close to him.

"Avery, how *great* to see you," Suzee said.

"Always," Avery said, resting a hand on Marcus's lapel.

"We're doing a segment on the leading women in media. Avery told me about the connection between you two, and that you were considering running a feature on Avery and Charm in *Stylish*."

"We're considering it," Suzee said dryly.

"Well, I think it would be great to include the process of you picking Charm in our segment," Marcus said. "Let's face it, Avery is very telegenic."

"Mar-cus," Avery scolded.

Just as Avery had anticipated, Suzee wasn't going to say no to *Timeline*. "Well, I think that sounds just fantastic!" she gushed.

"The next step is to schedule a time to shoot Avery coming into *Stylish* with the perfume."

"Can't wait. I'll tell my assistant to expect your call. Oh look, there's Martha Stewart, we're neighbors up in Westport," Suzee said, before taking off with a shouted "Martha!"

Avery watched her go with a satisfied smile. Revenge is sweet. And Charm's chances of success had just skyrocketed. "Thanks for that, Marcus," Avery said. She tried to step away from him, but he held tight.

"I like the way this feels," he said, lowering his voice.

Avery couldn't argue with that.

Marcus slid his hand down to the top of her buttock and said, "I like the way this feels even more."

Avery felt little sparks of electricity shoot through her.

"We do kind of fit, don't we?" Avery said, her own voice low and intimate.

"We always have."

Avery ran her hand down his cheek.

"Why don't we blow off this lunch," Marcus said. "I can get us a great corporate rate on a room here."

"What would your therapist say?"

"Do I have to tell him?"

"No. And anyway, impulse control is overrated," Avery said.

38

PATRICIA LUCAS'S NEW sublet was on lower Fifth Avenue in Greenwich Village, in a white brick 1960s building overlooking Washington Square Park. On the cab ride downtown, Avery was tense. She reminded herself that she had a lot to gain from this *People* article. In spite of her anger toward Patricia, as the cab pulled up in front of the building she felt an unexpected swell of pride: she carried a bottle of Charm in her purse and couldn't wait to show it off.

Patricia answered the door to her apartment wearing beige slacks and a white shirt with the sleeves turned back. Her face was expertly made up and her wrinkles had disappeared. Had she just been Botoxed? She smiled at Avery with the modesty and vulnerability that were her stock-in-trade as an actress. She looked as if she had somehow managed to turn the clock back to her prime.

"There's my darling daughter," she said in her soft warm voice.

"You look nice," Avery said.

"Thank you. It takes a lot of effort to look this effortless."

The apartment was expansive, with high ceilings, built-in book-cases, a terrace off the living room, and lots of windows. It was fur-nished with a mix of antiques and modern pieces and had a cozy, slightly bohemian feel, with a touch of glamour.

"Isn't this apartment heavenly? I had to smash the piggybank to pay for it, but it's an investment in my career . . . and yours."

They stood there for an awkward moment, with nothing to say to each other. Avery was hoping that Patricia would pepper her with questions about how things were going in her life. Nope.

Finally Patricia said, "You look wonderful, too." She turned away as a pained look flashed across her face. She looked around the apartment. "It's so funny, or sad, to think that I used to take this level of comfort for granted. I thought I would always live like this . . ." Her face grew wistful, even lost. She sat on a sofa and sighed deeply.

Avery softened. She was touched by her mother's admission, by her loss and remorse. It was the first time since they'd met that Av-ery didn't feel like she was watching a performance.

"I try to find the inner resources, the strength to meet the world again, but it gets harder each time," Patricia said. "This isn't my first attempt at a 'comeback.' I'm tired, I really am. A big part of me wishes I could buy a little house in Carmel or on Cape Cod, and just live a nice quiet life. But I can't. And it's no one's fault but my own."

Avery went to her, put a hand on her shoulder. "You can't think that way. We've all made mistakes. We have to keep moving forward. Come on, Mom, buck up."

Patricia looked up at Avery and said, "Do you realize that's the first time you've called me 'Mom'?" She took her hand and kissed it.

The doorbell rang. The spell was broken.

Patricia stood up, suddenly anxious, pulling herself together. "Oh dear, that must be Kitty. My manager." She checked herself out in a large hanging mirror, fluffed at her hair, leaned in close and examined her skin. Then she went and opened the front door.

"Hi, Kitty. This is my daughter, Avery. Avery, this is Kitty Mullen."

Kitty was somewhere in her forties. She carried a few extra pounds and wore enormous glasses, clunky jewelry, and too much makeup. There was something a little hard about her. She and Avery shook hands.

"Your mother is a major talent," Kitty said. "*Major*. And I'm going to make sure the world knows it." She eyeballed the navy suit and white silk blouse Avery was wearing. "That suit is a little too office-wear for tea with your long-lost mom. Did you bring anything else?"

"I didn't."

"You and Patricia are pretty much the same size. Patricia, do you have something a little less severe that she can wear?"

"Let's go look," Patricia said, taking Avery's hand and leading them into the bedroom.

Kitty opened the bedroom closet and cast a practiced eye on Patricia's wardrobe. She pulled out a powder blue blouse with a scooped neck. "This is perfect. We want to soften you."

"That blouse is *not* me," Avery said.

Patricia took the hanger from Kitty. She led Avery over to the full-length mirror and held the blouse up in front of her.

"See, darling, it looks wonderful with your coloring. And Kitty is right, we want to create a homey mood."

"These jeans are a great match," Kitty said, holding up a pair of crisp blue jeans.

"With those jeans and this blouse, I'll look like a country-western singer," Avery protested.

"And we haven't even teased your hair yet," Patricia cracked. She and Kitty laughed.

"Remember, this story isn't about Flair," Kitty said. "It's about a mom and her baby girl. It's inspiring, aimed right at the heart."

Avery changed into the jeans and blouse. Looking in the mirror, she had to admit that she felt comfortable and looked pretty, in an unassuming, back-porch way.

Patricia stood beside her and took her hand. "Thank you for doing this," she said.

"Sure. By the way, I brought along a sample of Charm, my perfume." Avery took the bottle out of her purse and handed it to Patricia.

"Oh, darling, how exciting!" Patricia gushed. Then she set the bottle down on the dresser top.

"Aren't you going to smell it?" Avery asked.

"Oh, of course! Silly me." Patricia opened the bottle and held it under her nose. "Oh, it's *lovely*." Then she recapped the bottle and put it back on the dresser top.

"I don't think we should clutter up the interview with too much information," Kitty said. "Remember, this is about your mom. We're trying to get her back into the public eye."

"So you don't think I should mention Charm?" Avery asked.

"I don't think there's any harm in mentioning it, once maybe, but let's not take the focus off Patricia Lucas's search for her daughter."

Patricia lowered her voice and said, "I'm sure this all sounds terribly selfish." That look of desperation appeared in her eyes.

"Don't worry, we'll keep the attention on you," Avery said.

"And on *us*," Patricia said.

"Now let's get the living room set up," Kitty said.

They arranged a love seat and armchair around a coffee table, making adjustments until the light from the windows was most flattering to Patricia.

Patricia and Avery sat side by side in another awkward silence, while Kitty went into the kitchen. She came back with a tray that held a teapot, two cups and saucers, and a plate of cookies. She set it down on the table and stood back.

"Perfect!" she declared.

"One more thing," Patricia said. She got up and turned on the CD player. "It's Mozart. He always puts me in touch with my best self."

The doorbell rang. Patricia tensed, closed her eyes, took three deep breaths, and mumbled something that sounded like a yoga chant.

Kitty answered the door.

"Hi, I'm Courtney Lynch, from *People*." Courtney was about thirty with an angular, intelligent face. "And this is our photographer, Phil Rockwell." He was older, stocky, all business.

As the women engaged in a bit of small talk, Phil set up his camera equipment. When he was ready, Courtney took out a tape recorder and a yellow legal pad. She sat in the armchair, turned on the tape recorder, and began.

"I must tell you, Patricia, that after I got this assignment I rented just about all of your movies. You're a wonderful actress."

"Why, Courtney, thank you," Patricia said. Avery noticed a subtle change in Patricia's demeanor. She sat up straighter, her jaw firmed up—she was going into performance mode.

"Why don't you tell me the story of your pregnancy with Avery."

Patricia tilted her head and nibbled on her lower lip—for just a quick scene-setting moment. "I was just eighteen . . . barely more than a child, really. I'd just arrived in Los Angeles and I had a silly fling with a silly boy—it was the seventies remember, and everyone did that sort of thing." She looked down at her lap and smoothed out her slacks even though they were already smooth. "Well, I got pregnant. I had no money, my family was very conservative, I couldn't tell them. A couple of friends urged me to get an abortion. I just couldn't. Then one of my girlfriends came up with an idea. She had a cousin who lived back east, in Pennsylvania, who couldn't have children. She and her husband wanted a baby more than anything in the world. My friend said they would love to take mine. With just one stipulation: I must never ever attempt to contact my child." Patricia made a funny sound in her throat, as if trying not to cry. "I insisted on coming east and meeting with the couple. They were good, solid people who desperately wanted a child. I could tell they would give my baby a secure home with a lot of love." She looked over to Avery, patted her knee. "Still, you can't imagine what a difficult decision it was. I really felt as if I had no choice. I came east for the last month of my pregnancy and lived with them. When Avery was born, they took her and I went back to Los Angeles. That day I flew back to California was the saddest day of my life."

Avery listened to all this with growing dismay. It wasn't the truth. Patricia had given birth to Avery in a ward in a Catholic hospital that specialized in out-of-wedlock births and had immediately given her up for adoption. She had no idea who would adopt Avery. And there was no agreement that Patricia would never attempt to contact her child. Patricia was spinning a fairy tale.

Avery tried to keep smiling, but it wasn't easy.

"Avery, how does it make you feel to hear all of this?" Courtney asked.

Patricia looked at Avery with a perfect poker face, giving her an encouraging smile. How could she just lie through her teeth like that, rewrite history to make herself look better, at the expense of Avery's feelings, Avery's struggle, Avery's truth?

There was a long, increasingly tense pause. Avery had a powerful urge to tell Courtney the truth, or even to call off the rest of the interview.

But neither of those choices would be smart. If she gave in to her anger, Avery would lose. She would be a victim of Patricia yet again. No way was she going to let that happen. She was going to turn this lemon into lemonade.

Avery took a deep, calming breath, and said, "How does it make me feel? It makes me appreciate the fact that women have more choices today. We make our own decisions. We even start our own companies. Hold on a sec. . . ."

Avery went into the bedroom and got the bottle of Charm.

She came back, sat down, and put the bottle on the coffee table. "This is Charm, my new perfume," she said. "I wasn't going to mention it in the interview, but Patricia *insisted*. I wanted to talk about her, but she was *adamant*. Weren't you, Mom?"

Patricia looked like she'd just swallowed a fish, but she managed a nod and a tight smile.

"I had no idea Flair was about to bring out a new perfume," Courtney said.

"Try it," Avery said.

Courtney dabbed a little on her wrists. "Oh, it's nice. So refreshing and sensual. We must get a picture of the two of you with the perfume. . . . Patricia, could you hold it?"

Patricia took the bottle, struggling to contain the small frown pulling down the corners of her mouth. "I'm so proud of Avery," she managed.

"It's a wonderful hook for the story: long-lost mother supports rising-star daughter," Courtney said. "Phil, can you shoot it so the perfume bottle really pops?"

Avery put her arm around Patricia and both of them smiled for the camera.

39

THE RHYTHMIC SWOOSH of the windshield wipers was soothing to Avery. The rain blurred the world outside into a watery dreamscape, and as she drove past New Jersey's factories and malls the weather matched the soft melancholy of her mood.

Avery was going home.

To see her mother.

So much had happened, was happening, that she felt emotionally overwhelmed. It was as if her body, soul, and heart simply couldn't handle any more and were shutting down, going into a fetal curl to protect her from further onslaught.

But this was a mission she needed to make. There were things she needed to say to Jackie Wilkins. Even if they didn't penetrate the boozy fog that had overtaken her brain.

Avery was content to be in the cocoon of travel, her life focused on reaching her destination. It was Saturday, and she had rented a car and gotten on the road without telling a soul. The casting session for the face of Charm was next week; she would be in the middle of a whirlwind of publicity. She treasured this day alone, when she could leave the city and all that it represented behind, and travel to the place that she had come from.

She reached the outskirts of Wilkes-Barre. After passing through a landscape of strip malls and fast-food restaurants, she entered the city itself. It all looked so gloomy in the rain: the empty storefronts, aluminum-clad houses, bars and pizza parlors. As a child Avery couldn't wait to get out of Wilkes-Barre, but today she was glad to be back.

To forgive.

And to make amends.

She reached the compact downtown, its proud granite and brick commercial buildings a reminder of the city's more prosperous past. Then she entered the working-class neighborhood she had grown up in. She passed landmarks from her childhood: her red-brick middle school, the candy store where she bought peanut-butter cheese crackers, the library where she would take refuge from home, devouring books and magazines that filled her head with visions of a bigger, better world.

Avery turned onto Mayflower Street. There was nothing special about the block. It was lined with small houses with dented siding and neglected front yards. She reached 9 Mayflower and pulled the car to the curb in front of the two-story white bungalow. She just wanted to the look at the house and remember. For better or worse, this block, this house, was where she had grown up, where the person she was today was formed.

Suddenly Avery needed to do more than just look. She got out of the car and dashed up to the front door through the rain. She could hear a television blaring inside. She knocked.

The door was opened by an adorable Asian girl of about five.

"Hi, are your parents home?" Avery asked with a smile.

There was a questioning call from the next room, in a language Avery didn't recognize. The little girl disappeared, leaving the door open. Avery looked into the cramped hallway. The walls were still the same light green, dingy and scuffed, and there was the same row of hooks, holding layers of inexpensive coats. She suddenly remembered smells: beer, whiskey, cigarettes, frozen French fries, Calgon Bouquet bath salts. And light, the soft forgiving evening light that filled her bedroom with comfort and hope. Then more memories tumbled out, long ago memories, from the early years: her mom laughing at her dad's operatic belches, the three of them watching *Cheers* together, the excitement when Dad's scratch-off lottery ticket won him five hundred dollars.

A squat old Asian woman with a round unlined face appeared. She looked at Avery with great curiosity, as if she were an alien creature.

"Hi, I'm sorry to barge in, but I grew up in this house and I was wondering if I could come in, just for a minute . . . to look around."

The woman looked at her with utter incomprehension.

Suddenly a girl of about twelve bounded down the narrow staircase. She had on hip-hugging jeans, a tiny pink T-shirt, and matching purple lipstick and nail polish. "Who are you?" she asked.

"My name is Avery and I grew up in this house. I'm just in town for the afternoon and I was wondering if I could take a quick peek around?"

The girl turned to her grandmother and explained in their native tongue. The older woman nodded. The girl turned back to Avery and said, "No problem."

Avery stepped inside. In the living room, the old woman and the little girl sat side by side on a sofa and went back to watching two plus-size women sell plus-size ensembles on the Home Shopping Network. Avery walked past them into the cramped dining room, which was filled with enormous wholesale-club packages of paper towels and cans of soup.

Past that was the kitchen. It still had the same gray linoleum floor and green Formica countertops.

Avery stood in the doorway and looked into the room that should be the heart of any home. In her home it had been the heart of darkness. It was her father's favorite place to slam Avery across the face or across the room for some imagined infraction of his so-called House Rules, illogical dictates that he made up on the spot. It held the small table where her mother would sit in a cloud of cigarette smoke with her bottle of Jack Daniel's, where she would greet her gentlemen callers in the years after Dad left. The men would knock on the back door and she'd let them in, offer them a drink, turn on the radio, and dance around in her cheap black negligee. Then they'd lurch into the living room and tumble onto the couch in a sloppy, grunting approximation of lovemaking. Other smells came back to Avery: sticky sweat, foul breath, dried semen. She felt a wave of nausea sweep over her.

"You okay, lady?" the girl asked.

Avery turned away from the kitchen. She was afraid she might faint.

"Wanna see my room?"

Avery nodded and followed the girl upstairs.

"The folks are at work. They work three jobs each," the girl said. "We're Laotian."

The girl led Avery into her old bedroom. The walls were painted light pink and covered with celebrity posters—the latest cute boys and slutty girls, Parker's pals. The room was messy, strewn with clothes, magazines, and makeup. An iPod was playing Justin Timberlake.

"So, was this your old room?" the girl asked.

"Yes."

"That's kinda weird. Does it look different?"

Avery nodded. And it felt different. Avery's childhood had been erased from the room, her pain and her hope buried deep beneath the pink paint, the posters, the years. Whatever she had hoped to find in this house, in this room, was long gone. She suddenly wished she had stayed in the car.

But no, maybe it was good—to see this, to understand that this house was just four walls and a roof. It wasn't a place where she could find some hidden key to her past, to understanding and closure and acceptance. Those things didn't live in the material realm.

"You sure you're okay?"

"Yes," Avery said. It was time to leave.

Heading down the walk to the car, Avery realized that she had, after all, found what she was looking for.

40

AVERY PULLED UP to the Rhinehart Home, a squat brick building in a better neighborhood across town. The area had once been where the gentry lived, but they had long ago moved to the suburbs, and the large old houses had been split up into apartments and offices. The Rhinehart Home was built in the 1950s by a prominent family with a retarded daughter. Its original mission was to provide a comfortable home for the mentally infirm. But, like all of Wilkes-Barre, it had seen better days.

Avery got out of the car, carrying her purse and a shopping bag, and walked up the path, under skies that were finally clearing. The entry hall was dingy, with a linoleum floor, a cottage-cheese ceiling, a few molded plastic chairs, and a small stand with brochures on blood pressure, exercise, and nutrition. The whole place was painted light gray and smelled like soggy cafeteria food, rubbing alcohol, and human decay.

There was a small office off the entryway. Mrs. Burnside, the house manager, sat at her desk engrossed in a book of acrostics.

"Hello, Mrs. Burnside."

"This is a surprise. Haven't seen you in a while," she said, reluctantly pulling herself away from her puzzle.

Mrs. Burnside was small and pinched, wore Sansabelt slacks and a cardigan. She was firm but fair with the men and women who were her charges. She'd seen them come and go, and wasn't about to get attached, but if someone had a toothache she made sure they got to a dentist.

"I want to see my mom," Avery said. "How is she doing?"

Mrs. Burnside kept a glass bowl of Swedish fish candies on her desk. She popped one in her mouth, and as she chewed her face grew serious.

"Seen her worse. Seen her better."

"Is she eating?"

"On and off. She has a private stash of Pringles under her bed."

"I brought her a few things today," Avery said, indicating her shopping bag.

"You know where her room is," Mrs. Burnside said, casting a glance at her puzzle.

"Thanks."

Avery walked down the hallway, past a half dozen old people in various states of mental and physical decrepitude. She smiled at them, but mostly got vacant stares in return. She reached room number 6 and knocked. No response. She knocked again.

"Jackie?" she called.

She heard movement from inside the room and then a wary voice. "Who is that?"

"It's me, Mom . . . Avery."

The door slowly opened a crack, and a sliver of Jackie's puffy, defeated face appeared. She cast a blank eye on Avery.

"Hi, Mom, it's me . . . can I come in a minute?"

There was a pause and then Jackie turned from the door, leaving it slightly open. Avery walked in.

The room was small and held a single bed, a dresser, and a table. Avery paid an extra $250 a month so Jackie could have a single. There was a sink in one corner and a television on the table. NASCAR was on, but the sound was turned off. The room smelled of Vicks VapoRub, sweat, and stale potato chips.

Jackie sat on the side of the unmade bed. She was wearing a housedress. She had a lumpy, rounded body and a pale face with thickened features. Her dark hair was cut short and sticking out willy-nilly from her head, and her eyes registered only a distant confusion. All in all, she looked like what she was: an understimulated, heavily medicated sixty-sixty-year-old woman suffering from Alzheimer's disease.

Avery felt sorrow lodge in the pit of her stomach. It was a feeling that came over her every time she saw her mother. For an instant she wanted to turn and leave, get into her car and get out of Wilkes-Barre as quickly as she could.

Instead, she went and sat next to Jackie on the bed.

"Hi, Mom," she said.

There was a small flicker of recognition, as if somewhere deep in her unconscious she knew who Avery was.

This close to Jackie, Avery could smell a ripe fleshy smell that she remembered from when she was a girl. It was her mother's smell. Avery found it oddly comforting. She reached into her shopping bag and took out a box of chocolates.

"I brought you some chocolates."

She handed her the box. Jackie slowly opened it and then stuffed three chocolates into her mouth at the same time.

"That's all right, Mom, no one is going to take away your candy.

I'll make sure of that. I also brought you come cashews. Remember how much you always loved cashews? And some nice shampoo, and hand cream, and powder. And here are some slippers for you, nice soft slippers. And a cardigan. Oh, and a bag of mints. You love your sucky-mints."

Avery placed her presents on the little table one by one.

"It's so good to see you, Mom. I've been thinking about you a lot lately, about us, about everything."

Avery took a hairbrush out of her purse. She brought it up to her mother's scalp and tenderly ran it through the wild hair. Jackie offered no resistance, and slowly her eyes half closed, like a cat when it's being petted.

"I wanted to come see you because there are some things I need to tell you," Avery began in a soft voice. "I know what happened now. I know you adopted me. And I remember all the love you gave me at first. You gave me so much love." A hush came over the room as Avery combed her mother's hair. "Then later, you tried to protect me from Dad, I remember that, too. You used to get between us, and then he would hit you instead of me. And then that day you told me to get out of Wilkes-Barre. Do you remember that day? When you came home from the hospital on crutches? You told me I was better than what was here. . . . You did the best you could, Mom, and I know how unhappy you were, how hard your life was. You were trapped . . . but you gave me permission to go, to leave you. You gave me so much. But I was ashamed of you. So ashamed. Sometimes I even pretended you were dead. You don't deserve that. You never lied to me," Avery said, thinking of Patricia Lucas. "You never ever pretended to be someone you weren't. You loved me so much . . . and I loved you so much. . . ." Tears began to roll down Avery's cheeks but she just kept brushing. "I'm so sorry, Mommy, I'm so sorry. . . ."

Jackie looked at Avery. From somewhere deep down it flickered in her eyes: a knowing, an understanding. She reached out and wrapped her arms around her child.

Avery let herself cry as her mother gently rocked her in her forgiving arms.

41

AVERY EASED THE cozy, fur-lined moccasins onto her mother's feet. Jackie wriggled her feet and smiled. It was the first time she'd smiled all day.

"Oh, you like those," Avery said.

"I like them," Jackie said. She stood up and walked around the room, swinging her arms. Avery laughed at her cocky walk.

Avery took most of Jackie's clothes to the laundry room. While they were in the machine, she cleaned her room from top to bottom and made the bed with fresh sheets she got from Mrs. Burnside. Then Avery took Jackie down the hall to the bathroom. She helped her undress, got her into the shower, and shampooed her hair. The physical intimacy felt awkward at first—the sight of her mother's aging, flaccid flesh—but Avery quickly relaxed. Soon she was humming as she soaped and scrubbed.

Avery helped her mother dress in a clean blouse, pants, and the new cardigan. Then she brushed her hair again. Finally Avery reached into her purse and took out a bottle of Charm.

"Mom, this is a new perfume that I made. In Paris, Mommy, in Paris, France."

Avery opened the bottle and held it under Jackie's nose.

"Pretty!" Jackie exclaimed.

Avery tipped the bottle up and dabbed some Charm on her mother's neck and the insides of her wrists. Jackie twitched her nose and smiled. Outside the window the rain had stopped and the sun was peering through the clouds.

"Would you like to take a little walk?" Avery asked.

Jackie nodded.

The air outside smelled after-the-rain fresh.

"How would you feel about moving closer to me?" Avery asked as they walked down the street toward a small playground.

"Move?" Jackie said, looking scared.

"Don't worry, it would be a good move. You see, my career is going pretty well—oh, there are so many things I want to tell you!—and very soon I might be able to afford to move you into a really nice place. A place where you'd have a pretty room and there would be singing and games and outings, where the food would be delicious, and where you would receive treatment. Your memory might even get better."

Avery kept up-to-date on the latest advances in Alzheimer's treatment and knew that there were drugs that were showing good results in some patients. There were wonderful assisted-living residences that provided medical care. They were expensive, but it was time for Avery to start paying herself a bigger salary, especially if it meant providing for her mother.

"Where do you live?" Jackie asked.

"I live in New York City, but I'd probably try and find a place for you in a nice suburb."

Avery and Jackie walked in silence for a little while, an easy silence.

It was late afternoon, and twilight licked at the horizon, softening the light.

"It's pretty out," Jackie said.

"Yes, yes, it is."

They reached the playground and sat on a bench. There were a couple of older children climbing the jungle gym, kids at the tail end of childhood. As Avery watched them, she thought of herself growing up across town. She wondered what kind of families waited for these kids at home. Or didn't wait.

A mother appeared, pushing her toddler in a stroller. They were out taking advantage of the clearing weather. The mom looked tired but happy as she lifted her daughter out of the stroller and set her down on the ground. The girl smiled and raced toward a tiny horse on a spring. She fell and started to cry. Her mom picked her up and cradled her, rocked her, stroked her head. Slowly the girl's crying subsided.

The mom looked over at Avery. They smiled at each other.

"They take the littlest things so hard sometimes," the mom said.

"She's an adorable girl."

"Thanks. I sure think so. Course I am her mom."

"It's not always easy being a mom."

"That's for sure. Both me and her dad work full-time, and some nights I'm just not in the mood. But, you know what—you do your best, right?"

"Mommy, Mommy, put me down!" the girl cried. She was fully recovered, raring to go.

Her mother put her down, and this time she made it to the tiny horse, clambered onboard, and happily rocked.

"I'm Avery, by the way, and this is my mom, Jackie."

"I'm Kristin. I've seen your mom around here."

"You have?"

"Oh sure. She's sad a lot. But today . . . today she looks happy."

42

MARC TANNER'S STUDIO was buzzing, filled with ten top models, a film crew, journalists and bloggers, the live podcaster, stylists, hair and makeup, ad agency people, and Justin and a crew from Flair. Infectious pop-rock music was playing, and an elaborate buffet was set out. Marc was in front of a large white backdrop, getting ready to take the girls' test pictures.

Avery was over in a corner of the studio, being interviewed on the live podcast by a young Internet journalist named Becky. "So what are you looking for in the model?" she asked.

"We're looking for a girl who is fun-loving, but serious about her goals, who is romantic and sensual, but most of all she has to have a certain . . . *charm*," Avery said with a smile.

Justin appeared. "Isn't this a blast?"

"This is Justin Fowler, the heart and soul of Flair," Avery said.

"More like the hands and feet," Justin said. He was in high spirits and looked dashing in an impeccable gray suit.

Suddenly the music stopped and Marc's voice boomed out over

the cacophony: "All right, people, it's time to find the face of Charm. Each model has three minutes. The poses are up to you—our only direction is to *charm us*. Turn that music back on and let's get started."

The first girl was stunning: tall and blond, very Gwyneth Paltrow. She struck her poses with poise and confidence, and she didn't have a bad angle. But she was a little too patrician, too cool, to be the face of Charm. The girl they picked had to be more down-to-earth and accessible.

"Thank you, terrific, *next*," Marc called.

The next girl was mixed race, with a slightly exotic beauty, a lithe toned body, and an electrifying smile. She had star quality for sure, and there was something about her racial mix that said "now" and even "the new All-American look." Her drawback was a certain knowing insouciance, a touch of irony in her eyes. It was intriguing, but a little bit too detached for Charm.

"You're fantastic, thanks so much, *next*," Marc called.

Avery was looking down at her notes. When she looked up, Parker was standing in front of the white backdrop, striking an exaggerated come-hither pose. She was wearing a gold lamé dress the size of a postage stamp and gold high-heel straps. Her hair was frosted and teased, she had on way too much makeup, and she looked gaunt and wild-eyed. There could be no doubt: she was flying high on some combination of booze, cocaine, and pills.

"Well, aren't you going to take my picture?" she barked at Marc.

A horrified hush slowly descended on the studio.

"I said *aren't you going to take my fucking picture?*"

There was absolute silence filled with razor-sharp tension.

Finally Marc said in a calming voice, "Parker . . ."

"Don't 'Parker' me, sweetheart!" She turned on Avery. "This is the last goddamn time you freeze me out of the picture. Did you think you could just stash me out in L.A. and keep me happy with your goody-goody phone calls about how proud you were that I was going to my meetings, you conniving little bitch! Well, guess what? Meetings are for losers—and Parker Adams is not a loser. I own Flair and everyone in this room works for me—including Avery High-and-Mighty Wilkins." She wheeled around and fixed on a petrified young assistant. "YOU! Yeah you, the dumpy chick with the cheesy haircut—bring me a soda RIGHT FUCKING NOW!"

The young woman grabbed a can of soda and brought it over to Parker.

"Good girl. You earn ten brownie points and the right to kiss my rich white ass." Parker popped opened the soda and took a long swallow. "Okay, let's get to work here. I'm casting the Charm girl and I'm not sure what I want, but I'll know it when I see it. I'm a total fucking professional and I have a brilliant eye, isn't that right, Avery? I have my pulse on the moment, right, Avery? Don't at look at me in that pitying way, you pathetic little white-trash toad. I don't want your pity, I want your respect. I demand your respect because I own you!"

Then she stopped cold and a terrible stunned dizziness washed over her face. Her eyes rolled up and she blacked out.

43

"IT'S A DISASTER, a fiasco," Justin said.

It was 8 A.M. the next morning, and he and Avery were sitting in her office watching as E! ran footage of Parker's meltdown. On the table in front of them was the *New York Post*, its headline blaring "CHARM FOOL!" The devastating images were all over the web, too; YouTube was getting a zillion hits on a video clip of the incident.

Avery got up from her desk and began to pace. "What are our options?"

"There aren't many and none of them are attractive. The key problem is that Flair and Charm will always be associated with this incident. We'll be the butt of jokes on Jon Stewart and Jay Leno, the web's latest whipping boy. That stain is very difficult to erase."

"I could kill Parker," Avery said.

"I'll hold her down," Justin said.

They looked at each other and almost managed a smile.

"You know, Avery," Justin said, growing serious, "I'd be very careful about Parker. I think she's crossed the line from self-destructive to just plain destructive. And she seems fixated, even obsessed, with you."

"You think I might be in danger?"

"I do think she's capable of violence of some kind. I hope I'm wrong, but we have to keep close tabs on her. Watch her behavior very carefully. Keep track of her whereabouts," Justin said. "She's desperate at this point. And desperate people do desperate things."

"There is no way I am going to let Parker Adams intimidate me. Fear is not my style. As for violence, if it comes to that, I will kill her."

"That's my firecracker," Justin said. Then he sighed and rubbed his chin. "I think we have to face the hard truth that we may not be able to salvage Charm after this debacle. I know it was going to be our signature product, and we have a lot invested in it, financially and in every other way, but in business it's important to know when to cut your losses. We can step back, come up with another perfume in six months, a year even. At that point all this publicity will turn out to be helpful—people will know who you are and will be paying attention."

"I love that perfume. My heart and soul are in it," Avery said.

"I know, and everyone else loves it, too. It was going to be huge."

Avery felt a touch of the nausea she'd been experiencing lately. She sat back down at her desk. "It is going to be huge. We're going to find a way out of this. I'm not going to let that sick, spoiled bitch take me down!"

There was a knock on the open door.

"May I come in?" Brad was standing in the doorway. He looked like he'd just tumbled out of bed—he hadn't shaved and had thrown on jeans and an old shirt—but he radiated determination and dynamism. Avery hadn't him seen since that night at Roseland. She immediately forgot about her nausea.

"Yes," Avery said.

He strode into the room. "I'm going to get right to the point. I have some experience in crisis management. Both professional and personal," he said, giving Avery a meaningful look. "And I have an idea of how to turn this Parker incident into a positive."

"I'm all ears," Avery said. He was so forceful and vigorous and . . . sexy.

"Ditto," Justin said.

"Here's the plan. Parker is in Lenox Hill Hospital. Avery, you go visit her this afternoon. We alert the media that after the visit you'll be holding a news conference. You make a statement about Parker's condition. Talk about how much you care about her, and the fact that she has a disease and needs help and support. Then announce that you've arranged for her to be admitted to Spring Hill, the most exclusive rehab in the East. I've already called them and secured a room. Then you personally drive her up to Spring Hill."

Avery leaned forward on her desk. Justin's eyes were lighting up.

"The goal is to turn this from a story of debasement and conflict into one of forgiveness and redemption," Brad continued. "If it works, Avery, you'll be seen as sympathetic, even noble. And, not incidentally, you'll be ten times more famous than you were yesterday. The result: Flair is America's most talked about brand and Charm is perfectly positioned for a breakout debut."

"It's brilliant," Avery said, standing up.

"It certainly is. I'll call our press agents and have them get to work," Justin said, halfway out the door.

"Schedule the news conference for four o'clock so the early news shows can cover it live," Brad called after him.

Suddenly the office was quiet.

Avery and Brad looked at each other.

She crossed to him.

"I don't know how to thank you for this."

"I do."

"Brad, this is about business."

"It's also about friendship," he said.

"You're a wonderful friend," Avery said, feeling the pull of his magnetism.

He reached up and cupped her face in his hand. She didn't resist.

"I'd like to be a friend with benefits. . . ."

"Oh, Brad, I don't know. . . ."

"This isn't about knowing, Avery, it's about feeling."

Looking into his eyes, she felt her doubts about what had happened that night in Seattle melt away. And even if some vestige remained, who cared?

They came together and their lips met. His stubble was rough, and she smelled his pine soap. She wanted this. She *needed* it. A man, a strong man. Pleasure . . . release . . . Brad . . .

"Just a moment," Avery whispered.

She crossed to the office door and locked it. She turned to Brad. He was looking at her with respect and tenderness and want.

He held out his arms and she went to him.

44

PARKER'S PRIVATE ROOM looked more like an expensive hotel than a hospital. There were thick drapes, masses of flowers, and a cozy seating area. But there was nothing hotel-like about the IV drip she was receiving for malnutrition and dehydration.

Avery approached the bed. Parker looked terrible: pale, gaunt, and spooked, as if she was in shock. Avery didn't care how bad she looked; her well of sympathy was dry. Parker's stunt at the audition was the last straw. Avery was there for one reason: to get what she wanted.

"How are you feeling?" Avery asked.

Parker gave a little shrug and then her eyes filled with tears and her face began to contort. Avery knew what was coming: a torrent of self-loathing, apology, and regret. She wanted to short-circuit it.

"Don't let yourself get worked up, please," she said, sitting in a chair next to the bed and squeezing Parker's hand. "Hear me out a minute. Just relax and listen."

Parker closed her eyes and sighed deeply. When she opened

them, she spoke in a soft hoarse voice. "I guess I've earned the right to shut up."

Looking at Parker lying on the deep luxurious pillows in a hospital room that must have cost thousands of dollars a day, Avery had a sudden urge to slap her, demand to know if she understood how much damage she had caused. But what she said was "I think you have to be very easy on yourself, Parker. The most important thing to remember is that addiction is a *disease*, not a character flaw. You need treatment, not recriminations."

"But I tried meetings . . ."

"Yes, and they worked for a while. From what I understand, it often takes more than one shot to get sober. So, I have a proposal for you."

"I ruined everything for Charm, didn't I?"

"The best thing for Charm would be you getting better. But let's not even think about business right now."

Parker pushed her hair back from her face, turned, and looked out the window. There was something about the gesture and the angle of her face that made her look just like her father, just like Finn. Avery felt that familiar stab of yearning and loss. And with it came a sense of responsibility for his daughter. Avery fought down the feeling. It was a trap, and she'd stepped into it once too often already.

"We all need help sometimes, Parker, and you need it now," Avery said, moving in for the kill. "I have a dear friend, and he's been able to book you into Spring Hill. It's one of the country's best treatment centers for addiction. It's in a beautiful setting up in Litchfield County. I think you should go."

"Do I have a choice?"

"I think it would be the best thing for your health, your career . . . your happiness."

Parker closed her eyes and nodded.

"I'd like to drive you up there myself."

Parker's eyes welled with tears. "Why are you being so nice to me?"

"Because I care about you."

45

BRAD AND JUSTIN were waiting for Avery out in the hallway, expectant looks on their faces.

"She agreed to go to Spring Hill, and I'm going to drive her up as soon as the doctors say she's strong enough to travel," Avery told them.

"That's terrific news," Brad said.

"Listen, it's a mob scene outside," Justin said. "Everyone from the New York Times to the Drudge Report is there."

"Well, it's what we wanted. How do I look?" Avery asked.

"Like a beautiful, compassionate woman," Brad said.

Avery reached out and squeezed his hand.

They rode down in the elevator. As they crossed the hospital lobby, they could see that the sidewalk outside was a crush of photographers, reporters, film crews, and bloggers.

The revolving door deposited Avery into a blinding, cacophonous sea of flashbulbs and shouted questions. She straightened her shoulders, walked up to the microphones, and began to speak:

"I've just met with Parker. She's resting, getting her strength back. She feels terrible about her behavior and knows that she needs help. I'm taking her to a rehabilitation facility myself. We would like to keep the name and the location of the facility confidential, for obvious reasons. I would ask the press to please respect Parker's privacy. What she needs now is treatment, not attention."

The shouted questions began:

"What drugs was Parker on?"

"I think we should all concentrate on moving forward. This is about healing, not toxicology," Avery said.

"Have her doctors released any word on her condition?"

"Her condition is stable."

"Will you cancel Charm?"

"I'm not thinking about business right now. Parker has a disease and she needs treatment. That's where all my energies are going right now."

"Has this destroyed Flair's image?"

"Flair is a lot more than one incident. We stand behind our products—and our people. They're all at work, doing their jobs. I'm very proud of them."

"Where is the treatment center?"

"How long will she stay there?"

"Did she have prescriptions for her drugs?"

Avery had accomplished what she wanted. She had set the tone for the coverage and established herself as Parker's caretaker. "Thank you all, I have to go now," she said. She stepped away from the microphones, and Justin and Brad led her through the crowd to a waiting car. The driver opened the back door and they ducked inside.

It was hushed in the back of the car; the windows were tinted, the seats deep and soft. Avery closed her eyes and rested her head against the buttery leather.

"You were pitch perfect," Justin said.

Brad took her hand and she rested her head on his shoulder.

As the car slowly made its way through the crush, Avery could hardly believe that it had come to this. When she founded Flair, she had wanted to prove to herself that she could build a successful company, a fulfilling career.

That was turning out to be the easy part.

46

AVERY LEANED OVER the toilet bowl retching a thin stream of bile. It was four-thirty in the morning and her denial was crumbling. She could no longer ignore her tender and swollen breasts, the light spotting, the sensitivity to certain smells, her missed period.

Avery knew that she was pregnant.

When there was nothing more to bring up and her stomach felt like it had been turned inside out, Avery stood up and looked at herself in the mirror. She looked like a ghost. Pale and haunted. Pale because she was sick. Haunted because she knew how complicated her pregnancy would be, how many hard choices she would have to make.

Still, she needed to know for sure. She had a home pregnancy test somewhere. She knelt down and rummaged through the vanity cupboard, found it buried in the back, under a hair dryer and a box of Q-tips. She checked the expiration date—still valid. She opened the kit, sat on the toilet, took out the stick, and urinated on it. Then she put it on the counter and waited. The minutes seemed to elongate, tick by in slow motion. And then there it was, coming in strong: a plus sign.

Avery went into her tiny kitchen and made herself a cup of tea. She took the tea and sat at her small café table and hugged her robe around her. It was time to face up to some very tough questions.

Was the father Marcus or Brad? They'd both worn condoms, but everyone knew that condoms weren't foolproof. Would she ask them each to take a DNA test to determine which one was the father?

Would she terminate the pregnancy? Would she be more likely to end it if Marcus was the father, or Brad? And could she really go through with an abortion?

If she didn't terminate the pregnancy, would she keep the baby? Could she bear to give it up for adoption?

If she kept the baby, would she raise it alone? Was she ready to commit to either man? And could she commit just because he was the father? More important, did she have what it takes to raise a child? Considering her role models of Jackie and Patricia, would she just intrinsically be a bad mother?

Could she run Flair and still handle a pregnancy and the demands of an infant? The timing was just so wrong. She imagined morning sickness and slogging through slush at seven months; then breast-feeding, sleepless nights, bone-deep exhaustion. Flair was her baby, too, and it still needed her undivided attention.

Avery sat there feeling overwhelmed, trying to sort things out. Pearly gray dawn light was filtering into the apartment. She walked into her bedroom, propped up the pillows, sat up in bed with her legs curled under her, and reached for the phone.

"Hello?" came the groggy voice.

"Justin, I'm so sorry to wake you up. . . ."

"Are you all right?" he said, instantly 110-percent awake.

"Yes. No. I don't know. . . . I'm pregnant."

There was a short pause.

"Accidental, I assume?"

"Yes."

"Tell me more."

"I just confirmed it with a test . . . and I don't know what to do."

"First of all, you know that you have a choice."

"Yes, thank God for that."

"Amen. What else?" Justin asked.

"I don't even know who the father is. That sounds awful, but the truth is it could be Brad or Marcus."

"And you're ambivalent about both of them."

"I'm not sure I'd want to raise a child with either one of them, even under the best conditions. And what does this mean for the company, and for Charm? Do I want to be a mother now, and of this child? I mean I live in a small apartment and work sixty-hour weeks, I travel all the time, . . . and . . ." Avery felt a sudden cold fear grip her spine, ". . . could I be a mother? It's such a huge responsibility, to a little defenseless life, what if I made some terrible mistake, what if I—"

"Stop right there. You're going down a dangerous path. I know you well enough to know that you would be a *wonderful* mother, Avery. You're considerate, you're smart, you're disciplined. Look at what a great mother you've been to Flair. You may be young and beautiful, but you have a maternal attitude towards your employees."

"Oh, Justin, you're so kind, but this is different."

"I know it's different, but I also know that you can handle it. We both know you've handled worse things than an unexpected pregnancy. I have *absolute* faith in you."

"What do you think I should do?"

"Nothing. I mean right now. You have a very full plate right now.

You're driving Parker up to Connecticut next week. You don't have to decide today, or even next week. Give yourself a little time. We'll keep talking, weigh all the pros and cons; the right answers will come to you."

"You're right, I don't have to decide today," Avery said, exhaling with a sigh, feeling her panic recede.

"No, you don't. And you have a twenty-four-hour sounding board right here."

"Get ready to do a lot of listening."

"Why don't I come over there and make you breakfast."

"I couldn't eat."

"You have to eat. And I make a mean bowl of oatmeal."

47

AVERY WAS SITTING at her desk. She had just made an appointment to visit an assisted living facility out in Queens that afternoon. It had a terrific reputation and a special wing for Alzheimer's patients. Since she had learned she was pregnant, her determination to get her mother into a good home close to New York had increased. As she weighed her options, she was thinking a lot about what it meant to be a mother. If she did decide to have the baby, she wanted to be prepared for motherhood, to shake her doubts that she wouldn't be up to the job, that her own background made her essentially unfit to nurture and raise a child. Part of this process was thinking about her own childhood. It would have been hard to call Jackie Wilkins a good mother, but in her own way she had tried. And whatever decision she made about the pregnancy, Avery had a powerful desire to take care of Jackie. Blood or not, she was family.

Sitting next to the phone on Avery's desk was a letter from Lucy that had arrived that morning. No doubt it was a weepy mea culpa. But here again the pregnancy was affecting her feelings. If she did have the baby, Lucy would be its aunt. In spite of her juvenile infatuation with Karl, Lucy was smart, kind, and had good intentions. She had proved that during the time she worked at Flair. Avery would love to be able to get her thoughts and feelings about the pregnancy.

She opened the letter and read:

Dear Avery,

I wanted to apologize in writing for my inexcusable behavior. You gave me an opportunity and I betrayed you. I'm very sorry.

I dumped Karl the next day. I'm so embarrassed that I fell for him. I wanted a man so badly that I literally lost my head. I obviously have a lot of growing up to do. As you said, I needed to learn this lesson. I'm just so sorry that it came at your expense, and at the expense of our relationship.

I got a new job—as a waitress! It isn't exactly a high-powered career, but I think I need to concentrate on getting my emotional life together right now. Besides, being around all that food is helping me lose weight!

I wanted you to know how terrible and sad I feel about what happened.

Love, Lucy

Avery felt her throat catch. Lucy's remorse was so sincere, and there was no self-pity in the letter. She was just a kid finding her way. Yes, she had made a big mistake, but she knew it and took responsibility. Avery remembered the vulnerability and eagerness in her eyes. She picked up the phone and dialed.

"Hello?" Lucy answered.

"Hi, it's Avery."

"Oh, hi," Lucy said in a tentative, hopeful voice.

"Thank you for the nice letter."

"You're welcome," Lucy said simply.

Avery was impressed again. Lucy wasn't getting all mushy. She had stated her apology but she wasn't belaboring it.

"Listen, I'm driving out to Queens this afternoon and your neighborhood is on my way. I wondered if you wanted to meet for a cup of coffee."

"I'd like that a lot, Avery."

"Terrific."

48

LUCY LIVED IN Williamsburg, an old Brooklyn neighborhood across the East River from Manhattan that had become popular with young people because it was still affordable. Lucy was waiting for Avery at a local coffeehouse, and she stood up as Avery approached her table.

"Hi," Lucy said.

There was an awkward moment. Should they hug? Avery settled for a kiss on the cheek.

"It's nice to see you," Avery said, sitting down. A waitress came over and Avery ordered a cappuccino. There was another awkward pause before she said, "So, you've got a new job."

"I do. At a little Italian restaurant a few blocks from here." Lucy took a sip of her coffee and looked Avery right in the eyes. "Do you want to talk about what happened with Karl?"

"No, I don't. I accept your apology and I want to move on. In fact, I want to invite you to the Charm launch party."

"Really?" Lucy asked excitedly. Avery nodded. "I would love to come."

The sisters smiled at each other.

"So, have you seen Patricia?" Lucy asked.

"Yes. We did an interview for *People* together, and she lied about the facts of my birth and adoption."

"Mom's always had a very shaky relationship with the truth."

"Well, this was *my life* she was talking about. Instead of letting me be who I am, she was trying to turn me into a character in her movie."

"You're angry about it, aren't you?" Lucy said.

"I sure am. She made it sound like she had given me up to some saintly couple."

"And she didn't?"

"She had no idea where I would end up. She left town the day after I was born. I grew up with an alcoholic father who abused me. He screamed at me. He hit me. He . . . touched me. He finally left, but after he did my mom really went downhill. She drank all day, took pills, and entertained strange men every night," Avery said.

Avery stopped suddenly and realized what she had just done. She had told Lucy the truth about her childhood. The words had poured out of her naturally. She had never told anyone except Finn before. She felt goose bumps break out on her arms. And then she felt light-headed, in a good way. And she felt free, like her body could float up to the clouds.

"Oh my God, Avery, I had no idea," Lucy said.

Avery looked at her sister's open face, filled with sympathy. "You're only the second person I've ever told. I've been so ashamed. In fact, I tell people that I'm from a nice middle-class background."

There was a pause and the coffeehouse seemed to grow hushed around them. "I'm honored that you told me," Lucy said. "And my admiration for what you've overcome is off the charts."

Avery felt her throat catch.

There was another pause, then Lucy took a sip of her coffee and rubbed her hands on her thighs. "But can I point out something that you might not want to hear?"

"Of course," Avery said.

"Haven't you been doing exactly what you're accusing Patricia of doing?" Lucy said. "Changing the facts to suit her image of herself?"

Avery was brought up short. Her cappuccino arrived and she didn't even notice. "You're absolutely right," she said finally, "that's exactly what I've been doing. But as of here and now, I'm going to stop!"

"You're amazing, sis."

"Lucy, you've given me a real gift today."

"I owed you one."

"It's true, you did."

They laughed. Avery took a sip of her cappuccino. "There was something else I wanted to talk about."

"Shoot," Lucy said.

"I'm pregnant."

Lucy's eyes opened wide. "Wow. Say more."

"The father could be either Brad or Marcus. And I'm not sure if I want to go through with the pregnancy. It's bringing up all sorts of intense feelings."

"You should know that whatever advice I give you is going to be prejudiced—I've always had a burning desire to be an aunt," Lucy said with a smile, reaching out and squeezing Avery's hand.

The words, the smile, the gesture were a balm to Avery. She had a sister she could share all this with.

"I think you should find out who the father is," Lucy said.

"Why?"

"Because he's a big part of the picture. It will affect your decision.

From what you've told me, Brad is a lot more mature than Marcus. And he's certainly able to provide for a child."

"But I'm not sure I'm able to provide for a child. And I don't mean financially. This feels like the wrong time for a lot of reasons," Avery said.

"Well, thank goodness women still have rights in this country," Lucy said. "But I still think you should find out who the father is."

"You're right. I just couldn't imagine raising a child with Marcus. He's still a kid himself. So I'd need to do a DNA test," Avery said.

"How far along are you?" Lucy asked.

"I'd say eight or nine weeks."

"Well, it's too early for amnio, but you can do chorionic villus sampling," Lucy said. "I learned about it in biology last semester. They take a tiny piece of tissue from the placenta to determine the baby's DNA."

"But I'd still need DNA from either Brad or Marcus to see if there's a match. And I don't want to tell either one of them I'm pregnant yet. It's my body and I don't want them complicating my decision."

"Well, you need some blood from one of them. Do you think you can figure out a way to get it?" Lucy said.

"Yes," Avery said, her wheels starting to turn, "I probably can."

49

THE BAYSHORE SENIOR Living Home sat on a hill overlooking Long Island Sound. It was an attractive three-story building with balconies and dormers. Avery had just finished her tour and she was impressed. The rooms and apartments were large and cheery, the dining room was inviting, there was a beauty salon, an exercise room, and the staff was knowledgeable and committed. There was a nurse on duty 24/7 and a special, individualized program for Alzheimer's patients. The care was clearly superb, and the residents she met raved about the place. It was expensive, but it was worth it. Avery would feel secure knowing that Jackie was in such good hands, and less than an hour from Manhattan. She reserved an apartment for her mother.

Avery stood on the lovely landscaped lawn, took out her cell phone, and called the Rhinehart Home in Wilkes-Barre.

"Hello."

"Hi, Mrs. Burnside, it's Avery Wilkins. May I speak to my mother, please."

"Hold on, I'll go get her. Oh, by the way, Avery, Jackie has been better since your visit."

"Really?"

"Yes. She's been more responsive, and even cheerful at times. Hold on, I'll get her."

As Avery waited, she felt a wave of nausea. She put a hand on her stomach and gently rubbed it.

"Hello?" came Jackie's monotone.

"Hi, Mom, it's Avery."

"Hi, Avery." Her voice brightened.

"Listen, Mom, I found a wonderful new home for you."

"Okay."

"It's close to me and it's beautiful and I think you'll be happy there," Avery said.

"Okay."

"You'll be moving in two months."

"Moving?" Jackie sounded scared.

"Yes, Mom, moving to your new home. I'll come down and see you in a few weeks and tell you everything. I just wanted to let you know."

"Okay."

"I love you," Avery said.

"You do?"

"Yes, Mom, I do."

There was a long pause and then Jackie said, "I love you, too."

As she drove back into Manhattan, Avery called Dr. Claire Mead, the Upper East Side gynecologist/obstetrician that Justin had found for her.

"Dr. Mead's office."

"Hello, my name is Avery Wilkins and I'm pregnant and I'd like to make an appointment to see Dr. Mead."

"All right. The earliest the doctor has is next Friday afternoon."

"It's something of an emergency. Can she possibly see me this week?" There was a pause. "I'd really appreciate it."

"All right, I think we can fit you in at the end of the day on Thursday."

As she crossed the Fifty-ninth Street Bridge, Avery began to prepare herself for her big day tomorrow. She was driving Parker up to the rehab facility.

50

IT WAS A perfect day. The sky was scrubbed a deep blue, the air fresh, the whole world sparkling in the sun. Avery had just gotten off the thruway and was driving Parker to Spring Hill along country roads, through some of the loveliest scenery she had ever seen: gentle green hills dotted with fat cows and happy horses, old stone walls, ancient oaks, rambling white clapboard houses surrounded by gardens, tennis courts, pools. It was paradise.

"I fucking hate Connecticut," Parker said, lighting a cigarette. "Nothing but a bunch of boring old WASPs up here." Still gaunt after a week in the hospital, she was wearing enormous dark glasses, a short leather coat over a silver minidress, and rhinestone-studded flip-flops.

The tension in the car was thick, but Avery was determined not to let herself be goaded by Parker. The visit to the hospital and the press conference had accomplished their goals. Just as Brad had predicted, the tone of the media coverage had changed overnight, become sympathetic. Everyone seemed to be rooting for Parker to get better, and for Avery and Charm to succeed. Once Avery had delivered Parker to Spring Hill, a statement would be released stating that she was safely in an undisclosed rehab. Then she would be out of the way as they geared up for the Charm party. Mission accomplished. All Avery had to do now was deliver her to Spring Hill.

"So, what do you think this place will be like?" she asked.

"Like a convent with better towels. Lots of meetings, counseling, shit like that."

"What are the meetings like?"

"People talk about all the fucked-up things they did when they were loaded. They talk about their families, their feelings."

"Do you talk much?"

"Yeah . . . nah . . . depends on my mood."

"What do you say?"

Parker took a long drag of her cigarette and looked out the window. "Sometimes I get really bitchy, like saying I'm rich and it really doesn't matter how much trouble I get into because I'll always be taken care of."

"That's honest at least."

"Yeah, but it's a cop-out. Even I know that. Believe me, there are a lot of rich people who are totally miserable. Like my mother."

"Have you heard from her this week?"

"No. But she sent flowers every day," Parker said bitterly. "She doesn't even like me. She didn't want kids, she actually told me that. She only had me to make sure my dad wouldn't leave her."

At the mention of Finn, Avery felt her pulse quicken. "Were you and your father close?"

"I loved my dad."

"Your father was the most wonderful man in the world," Avery said. "He was smart, generous, brave, and he loved life. He talked about you a lot."

"Yeah, sure."

"He did. You were his little girl."

Parker looked sad for a moment. Then she tossed her cigarette out the window. "You know, Avery, you must think I'm really stupid. I know exactly what you're doing here. You're trying to manipulate me into being a good girl. You and my father had a *business* relationship. Don't feed me all this bullshit like you actually knew him."

"Actually, I knew your dad pretty well."

"What's that supposed to mean?"

"It means that I'm trying to care about you, Parker, but as usual you're making it really hard."

"Don't make me laugh. You hate me, Avery, and you want me out of the picture for the Charm launch."

"Well, do you blame me? You've been trying to destroy my company for the past two years. I'm not going to let it happen."

"We'll see about that."

"Is that a threat?"

Parker went silent. She lit another cigarette and a devious grin played at the corners of her mouth.

Avery saw a sign for Spring Hill and she turned down a long drive lined with tall trees. They passed sweeping lawns, flower beds, and a pond that had a pair of swans gliding across it. They reached an enormous old white house with more recent wings built onto either side. The place could have passed for a fancy country hotel.

As Avery parked in the circular drive, Parker pulled out her cell phone and dialed.

"It's me," Parker said into the phone, lowering her voice and shooting Avery a look.

Avery got out of the car. Parker sat there talking intensely on her phone.

A middle-aged woman immediately came out of the front door. She was handsome, with gray hair in a stylish cut, wearing a beige pantsuit.

"Hello, I'm Dr. Margery Collins, the director of Spring Hill," she said.

"Avery Wilkins, a pleasure." They shook hands.

"And that must be Parker," Dr. Collins said. She opened the passenger door. "Patients aren't permitted to have cell phones," she said firmly, holding out her hand.

Parker turned away from her and kept talking.

"Give-me-that-phone," Dr. Collins said.

"Who are you, the Wicked Witch of the West?" Parker said.

Dr. Collins didn't react.

Parker flipped the phone closed and handed it to her. "I was done anyway," she said in triumph.

"Welcome to Spring Hill," Dr. Collins said.

Parker slithered out of the car and looked around. She seemed to like what she saw, and for a moment Avery grew hopeful that she would really commit to getting better. Then Parker turned to Dr. Collins and asked, "What time are cocktails?"

51

AS SHE DROVE away from Spring Hill, Avery called Justin on her cell.

"Well, I dropped her off," she said.

"How did she seem?"

"Like Parker."

"I don't like the sound of that."

"I didn't either."

"Are you holding up all right?"

"I'm just putting one foot in front of the other. Who was it who said that ninety-nine percent of life is just showing up?"

"It was either Plato or Woody Allen, or maybe both. How are you feeling about your pregnancy?"

Avery hesitated. "I think maybe the time isn't right. . . ."

"Okay . . ."

"But that's not written in stone, or even in sand. But I do feel that if I take on one more thing I might collapse under the weight of it all—and having a baby is a *big* thing."

"It is a big thing. But on a strictly practical level, you do know that sales are strong. You can afford a bigger apartment and to hire all the help you need."

"Are you trying to complicate my life?"

"No, but this decision should be an informed one," Justin said.

"If I do have the baby, will you be its dad?"

"I have to go, I have an urgent meeting with the coffeepot." They laughed. "I will definitely consent to be the surrogate uncle and supply fabulous presents, Broadway shows, museum trips."

"Yankee games?"

"There *are* limits."

"So, is everything on track for the party?"

"Yes, and interest from the media is scorching. Brad's plan was beyond brilliant. We owe him big-time."

"We do."

"You know that I'm the soul of discretion—not—so how's it going between you two?"

"I would say things are fluid."

"I assume he doesn't know about your pregnancy?"

"I told Lucy," Avery said. "Three people in the world know, and I want to keep it that way."

"Gotcha."

52

DR. CLAIRE MEAD'S roomy, well-appointed practice was on a cross street off Park Avenue. After Avery had filled out a medical history questionnaire, a nurse led her into an exam room. She took her blood pressure, assured her that Dr. Mead would be with her shortly, and then left Avery sitting on the exam table. As soon as the door was closed, Avery, her heart thumping in her chest, got down from the table, opened the cabinet over the sink, and found what she was looking for: small glass vials. She quickly secreted two in her purse. Then she sat back on the exam table and folded her hands on her lap.

There was a knock on the door and Dr. Mead walked in. She was in her mid-thirties, tall and attractive with shoulder-length blond hair.

"Dr. Claire Mead," she said, extending her hand and smiling.

"Avery Wilkins."

Dr. Mead nodded in recognition. "So, tell me what I can do for you."

"I'm pregnant."

"Yes?"

"And the father could be one of two men," Avery said.

Dr. Mead didn't bat an eyelash.

"My decisions on the pregnancy depend, to some extent, on which man is the father," Avery said. "So I want to find that out."

"I see," Dr. Mead said.

"I'd like to do DNA testing on the fetus. Will you help me?"

"Yes."

"Thank you."

"You're in your first trimester?"

Avery nodded.

"Chorionic villus sampling carries some risk of a miscarriage. If you wanted to wait until your second trimester, we could do amniocentesis."

"I don't want to wait," Avery said.

"All right. I'll need to examine you, run some blood tests, and get a full medical history."

"And then how soon can you schedule the procedure?" Avery asked.

"Assuming all goes well, next week. You do know that in order to determine if there's a DNA match you'll need a blood sample from one of the potential fathers?"

"How much blood do you actually need?"

"Well, if the lab is drawing the blood, they usually take a full syringe. But all they really need is a few drops."

Just a few drops, Avery thought.

When she got out on the street, Avery took a deep breath and called Marcus.

"Yes?"

"Hi, Marcus, it's Avery," she said in a low voice.

"What a pleasant surprise."

"How are you?"

"Lonely," Marcus said.

"I'm a little lonely myself."

"Well, why don't you come over tomorrow tonight and then we'll both be a little less lonely."

"That sounds like a good idea."

"How does eight sound?" Marcus asked.

Avery thought of the vials in her purse, smiled to herself, and said, "Eight sounds perfect."

53

IT WAS EARLY evening and Avery and Justin were in the office. There were a thousand and one details to nail down for the Charm launch party, which was going to be held on a large sailing yacht berthed at the South Street Seaport. The location, the boat, the look—pale rose was the color theme—were all designed to send a message of timeless modern romance. The party was generating a lot of excitement, the media would be there in full force, and celebrities and socialites were clamoring for invitations.

"Roses are a no-brainer, but how about lilies of the valley, too? The smell is just so intoxicating," Justin said.

"I love lilies of the valley," Avery said.

"How are you feeling?"

"Funny you should ask. I have this sudden intense craving for a pint of Chunky Monkey."

"Your craving is my command. Besides, we need a little break. Back in a few," Justin said, heading for the door.

"Oh, Justin?"

He turned. "Yes?"

"I have to meet someone at eight tonight. Will you call me on my cell at eight-thirty? Make up some emergency in the office and tell me that I need to come in right away."

A look of intense curiosity came over Justin's face, but then he shrugged and said, "Don't ask, don't tell."

Justin left and Avery's phone rang.

"Avery Wilkins."

"This is Dr. Margery Collins, the director of Spring Hill."

"Oh, hi."

"I'm calling to let you know that Parker Adams's behavior has been troubling. In her therapy sessions, she's exhibiting an obsession with you. We're seeing a lot of rage. We're concerned that it could lead to some kind of acting out."

"Such as?"

"Well, Parker doesn't have a history of violence, except towards herself, but that doesn't mean we can rule it out," Dr. Collins said.

"But she's up in Connecticut," Avery said.

"For the moment."

"So you really think I may be in danger?"

"It's a real possibility. It's probably not imminent, but it's something to take very seriously."

"What do you suggest I do?"

"You might want to consider informing the authorities, perhaps applying for a restraining order," Dr. Collins said.

"I appreciate your call. If Parker gets any worse or if she makes any explicit threats, please let me know right away," Avery said.

"Of course."

After she hung up, Avery was hit with a sudden attack of complete exhaustion. Her body was definitely going through some changes. She lay down on the office couch and closed her eyes. That phone call was worrisome, but she had more pressing things on her mind. If she could just get a short nap, she'd feel better. She was dozing off when there was a knock on her open door. She opened her eyes to see Patricia Lucas standing in the doorway.

"Hello, darling," Patricia said in a soft voice.

Avery sat up on the sofa. "Patricia . . . hi."

"I'm sorry to interrupt your nap."

Avery stood up, wide awake. "No problem."

The two women didn't kiss or hug. The chill between them was palpable.

"I haven't heard from you since our tea," Patricia said in a wounded voice.

"I've been busy," Avery said. She went and sat at her desk.

There was a tense pause and then Patricia said, "Well, I've been hearing all about the Charm launch party. It certainly sounds very exciting."

"I hope it will be."

". . . I haven't received my invitation yet."

"The guest list is very tight, *everyone* wants to come."

"Including your mother."

"My birth mother."

"Darling, what is that supposed to mean?"

"It means that you didn't raise me, and you only established contact when it was in your own best interests. Then you tried to exploit me to jump-start your career."

"I think you're being a little bit naïve. That's the way the world works, Avery, take it from your mother."

"The only thing I'll take from you is an apology."

"You know my circumstances."

"Well, maybe you're in them *because* of the way you treat people."

There was a pause and Patricia's eyes welled with tears. "You're so hard on me, Avery."

"That's right, Mom, play the sympathy card."

The tears stopped.

"I've already told my publicist I'm going to be at the party," Patricia said. "He's going to get it mentioned in the gossip columns."

"That's a little bit premature."

"Are you telling me I'm not going to get an invitation?" Patricia said.

Avery looked her right in the eye. "Yes."

Patricia threw back her shoulders, strode over to the desk, and spit out, "That is the most hard-hearted and vindictive thing I've ever heard of!"

"You want to see what hard-hearted looks like? There's a mirror on the back of that door."

"You're really going to do this to me? Just freeze me out?"

"I'm surprised you're bothered by the cold," Avery said.

"Why, you . . . you . . . *bitch!*"

"If you'll excuse me, I have an awful lot of work to do."

Patricia turned and stormed across the room. When she reached the door, Avery said, "Oh, Patricia?"

Patricia stopped and turned, said a hopeful "Yes?"

Avery ran her fingers through her hair, shook her head in triumph, smiled, and said, "Let's do lunch."

54

AS AVERY RODE up in the elevator to Marcus's apartment, her pulse was racing. She opened her purse and double-checked that she had the little glass vials that she had taken from Dr. Mead's office.

Marcus answered the door still wearing his suit from work, and they gave each other a short kiss.

"Come on in, I just got home myself," he explained, pulling off his tie and shedding his jacket.

Avery sat on the couch in the living room and Marcus disappeared into the kitchen. The apartment was disheveled, as always. He could afford a cleaning person, but he preferred to live like a teenager.

"Red or white?" he called.

"White."

Marcus appeared carrying the bottle of wine and two glasses, which he set on the coffee table. "Brutal day," he said as he opened the bottle.

"I hear you," Avery said.

"Do you ever want to just chuck it all and move to an island somewhere?"

"Sometimes. But I get over it pretty quickly," Avery said.

"We'd be bored in five minutes, wouldn't we?" Marcus said. "We're two of a kind, aren't we, Avery?" She smiled. He poured two glasses of wine and handed one to Avery. She took a sip. Marcus drank his in one gulp and poured himself another.

"How's therapy?" Avery asked.

"I quit. No time. Man, I'm fried."

"Listen, we're both a little worn out, why don't we take a nice hot shower?" Avery said, crossing her legs.

"Together?" Marcus said, a glint in his eye.

"Why not?"

"That sounds like a very good idea to me."

Marcus grabbed the wine bottle and headed down the hall toward his bedroom. Avery opened her bag, took out the vial and her cell phone, and slid them into the pocket of her slacks. Then she picked up her wineglass and followed Marcus.

The bed was unmade and the sheets looked a little dingy. As Marcus started to take off his clothes, Avery headed right into the bathroom. The sink was behind the door, out of Marcus's line of vision. She poured the rest of her wine down the drain and then dropped her wineglass on the floor.

"Damn," she cried.

"What happened?" Marcus called.

"I broke my wineglass. No big deal, I'll pick it up." Avery knelt down and carefully picked most of the broken glass, making sure to leave a couple of shards. Then she slipped out of her skirt, blouse, and bra. She turned on the shower and steam began to fill the room.

Marcus walked in, naked. What a bod. But Avery's mind was on other things.

"Mmmm, this was a great idea," he said with a tipsy grin, taking in her breasts.

Avery kissed him, leaning back against the wall. He stepped forward.

"Shit!" he said, breaking the kiss and looking down. He turned up his foot. There was a small shard of glass sticking out of his sole.

"Oh, honey, I'm so sorry," Avery said. She knelt down and deftly pulled out the glass. Then she squeezed the area and fat drops of blood fell to the floor. "This doesn't look too bad. Why don't you hop into the shower and wash it off while I clean this up."

"Okay," Marcus said, stepping into the steamy stall.

He was facing away from her, lathering up. Her heart pounding, she took the vial from her slacks pocket, took out the stopper, used the shard of glass to push the drops of blood into the vial, and put the stopper back on. Then she slipped it back into her pocket. She grabbed a handful of tissues, wet them, and wiped up the blood and any leftover glass.

"All done," Avery said.

"Get that body in here," Marcus said.

Avery slipped out of her panties and stepped into the shower. Marcus turned to her, his anticipation showing.

Just then her cell phone rang.

"Oh shit," Avery said.

"Don't answer it," Marcus protested.

"I have to. My lawyer said he might call, I have to give him a yes or no on a contract issue, it'll only take ten seconds." Avery kissed him. "Don't go anywhere."

She stepped out of the shower and fished her phone out of her slacks pocket.

"Hello?"

"Avery, it's Justin, we have a crisis. The yacht hit a reef down in the Keys and won't be fixed in time to sail north for the party."

"Oh no," Avery said. "I'll be right over."

"What is it?" Marcus asked, his voice deflating.

Avery opened the shower door, a stricken look on her face.

"The yacht we booked for the Charm party hit a reef down in Florida. I've got to get back to the office pronto. You stay in there, I can find my own way out."

"But, Avery, what about . . . ?" he asked dejectedly.

"You're going to have take care of that yourself," she answered, already out the door.

55

AVERY LAY WITH her robe open on the exam table. Dr. Mead and a nurse stood over her. The vial with Marcus's blood was on a nearby countertop.

"All ready?" Dr. Mead asked. Avery nodded. The doctor dabbed a spot on Avery's abdomen with a numbing agent, then injected the local anesthetic. Then the nurse rubbed petroleum jelly over Avery's stomach.

Dr. Mead picked up the ultrasound wand and ran it over Avery's belly. They both looked at the monitor. There was the embryonic life growing inside her.

"Oh look," Avery gasped, feeling a stab of pure maternal instinct. Dr. Mead smiled at her.

The nurse took the ultrasound wand from the doctor. Dr. Mead picked up a long needle. "You may feel a little pinch," she said.

Avery closed her eyes as the doctor inserted the needle into her stomach.

"All done," Dr. Mead said.

"That was fast," Avery said.

"It doesn't take long. You may have a little bit of soreness when the anesthetic wears off, but it should go away quickly. We'll have the results in three to five days."

When Avery got outside, it was a beautiful evening—warm and dry with a comforting breeze. She decided to walk home, across Central Park. When she reached Bethesda Terrace, she stood beside the Angel of the Waters fountain and looked across the lake to the Boathouse. Where she had first met Brad. He had been sending her flowers twice a week, but not calling. The message was: *I'm here, but I'm going to give you all the space and time you need.* His instincts were perfect. If he turned out to be the father, she would be much more likely to have the baby. He was older, responsible, seemed to have reached a stage in life where he was ready to commit to a child. After the trauma of his wife's death, Avery sensed that he yearned for the stability and structure that parenthood demanded.

Avery took out her cell phone and dialed.

"Hello."

"Hi, Brad, it's Avery."

There was a short silence before he said, "It's nice to hear your voice."

"It's nice to hear yours."

"How's everything going with the Charm release?"

"Oh that."

They laughed.

"It's going fine," Avery said. "I hope you're coming to the party."

"Wouldn't miss it."

There was a pause.

Avery lowered her voice and said, "Thank you for the flowers."

"My pleasure."

"I want to see you soon . . . just not quite yet," Avery said.

"You know how to reach me," Brad said in a voice tinged with disappointment.

Avery hung up. She looked up at the Angel of the Waters and said, "I'm counting on you, kiddo."

56

IT WAS TUESDAY morning. The Charm launch party was on Friday night. Avery was standing in her kitchen drinking a cup of coffee and eating a banana before she left for the office. The phone rang.

"Hi, it's Dr. Mead."

"Good morning," Avery said.

"The DNA results are in from the chorionic villus sampling and the blood you gave us. They match."

"I see," Avery said, feeling her stomach hollow out.

"Are you all right?" Dr. Mead asked.

". . . Yes . . ."

"If you want to come in and talk to me, just let me know. I'm here."

"Thank you, Doctor."

Avery hung up and sat down. Marcus was the father. She felt numb. But it only took her a few moments to make her decision.

She was going to terminate the pregnancy.

Marcus was the wrong man. He was immature and showed no

signs of wanting to grow up. Parenting a child with him was out of the question. She could see it now: he would be there for the fun and easy parts, and AWOL for the tough stuff. And she just didn't want to be tied to Marcus for the rest of her life.

She ran over the other arguments against having the baby. It was the wrong time in her life. Avery wanted a baby *after* she was settled into a secure relationship. She wanted to plan for her baby, to partake in all the prenatal rituals with the father. And she wanted to take six months off after the birth, which was impossible right now. Having a child should be a joyous experience—one that's savored, not sandwiched in.

And then there was that terrible little voice that continued to haunt her. The one that told her she would be a *bad* mother. That she just didn't have what it took to nurture a baby and to raise a confident and independent child. After all, look at her role models—Jackie and Patricia. They were both failures as mothers. Would she continue their legacy? Try as she might to push these doubts aside, they continued to trouble her.

If she had a baby now, particularly this baby, she would be conflicted and maybe even resentful of the child. That wouldn't be healthy for either one of them.

As she swallowed her daily vitamin, Avery could almost ignore that little tug of guilt about her decision.

She picked up her bag, and headed out for the office. It was a muggy, uncomfortable day with a low gray sky. Avery reached the corner of Broadway and was about to cross when a dark van screeched to a halt in front of her.

That's odd, she thought.

The side door flew open and a man wearing a ski mask leapt out. He had a rag in his hand and he clamped it over Avery's face.

Then everything went black.

57

WHEN AVERY REGAINED consciousness, she was sprawled on the floor of the van, blindfolded. First she noticed the smells: grease and gasoline. Then she heard and felt the whish and thump of the tires on the road. She moaned, realizing that she had a pounding headache. She had no idea how long she'd been out. The last thing she remembered was the smell of the ether-soaked rag. She tried to move, but her wrists and ankles were bound.

Only one person could be behind this: Parker. Avery remembered her surreptitious phone call on the drive up to Spring Hill, and the warning call she got from Dr. Collins. She knew Parker was angry and disturbed, but this was psychotic. And she wasn't going to get away with it.

Avery lay there for the next hour as the van sped farther and farther from the city. Her captors were silent. There was just the occasional lighting of a cigarette, and then the smoke would singe her nostrils and make her headache worse. Avery had time to think. She had to stay alert and stay cool. Try to psyche out her kidnappers. Watch for an opening and then seize it.

Finally a nasal male voice barked, "Take this exit."

They drove for another half hour, at a slower speed. The driver turned on a heavy-metal radio station. That didn't do anything for her headache. When the song ended, a newscaster came on. "We have breaking news: Avery Wilkins, the founder of Flair Cosmetics and archrival of famous party girl Parker Adams, was kidnapped on a Manhattan street corner this morning—"

"Turn that fucking thing off!" the nasal voice ordered.

After another ten minutes or so, the van pulled to an abrupt stop. The side door was yanked open and the man grabbed Avery's upper arm and pulled.

"Come on, sweetheart, make like a bunny," he said.

Avery struggled to gain her balance, but it was impossible with her ankles tied together. She tumbled onto asphalt and felt a stabbing pain in her right knee. The man cursed and hauled her to her feet.

The driver's door slammed and then she heard another voice, this one with a strong Bronx accent.

"You moron, you can't even get her outta the van without messing her up?"

"She fell—whaddya think, I pushed her down on purpose?"

"Look at that blood—wipe her off, you pathetic fuckup."

"Don't call me a pathetic fuckup, you sick freak."

Avery felt a rag being wiped on her knee, which was starting to throb. But she'd learned something important: her captors were sloppy, cranky, and not too smart.

Suddenly there was a loud whirling noise in the sky that Avery recognized as a helicopter. It grew louder, then deafening, and then there was a sharp gust of propeller blowback. The helicopter had landed nearby.

One of the men grabbed Avery's legs, the other her torso, and together they carried her under the whirring blades and loaded her into the helicopter, pushing her into the space behind the backseat. Then they climbed in after her.

"Everybody in?" the pilot asked.

"We're in, we're in."

"Take off already, this thing is making me nervous."

The helicopter took off with a loud whoosh and began a stomach-churning ascent. Avery was thinking: Her kidnapping was on the radio, so there must have been witnesses. The police were looking for her. But had these thugs left a trail?

They were in the air for about an hour when the helicopter began its descent. It landed with a jolt and Avery was roughly unloaded. She was hustled away from the copter just as it took off again.

She was alone with her two kidnappers. But where were they?

58

THE FIRST THING Avery noticed was the air: it was incredibly fresh and pure. Then she heard the gentle lap of water. They were on a lake somewhere.

"Let's bring her in already," the guy with the Bronx accent said.

"Whaddya think, we were gonna leave her out here?"

The two men half-carried, half-dragged Avery across scruffy grass, up two steps, and inside.

It smelled like a rustic cabin: musty and mildewed, with undertones of strong coffee and fresh-caught fish. The men lifted Avery onto a bed. It was narrow, rickety, with a lumpy mattress covered by a scratchy wool blanket. Then they went back outside.

When the copter was out of earshot, Avery noticed something. The quiet. She couldn't hear any distant whir of tires on a highway, no lawnmowers or radios or outboard engines. It was the deepest quiet she had ever experienced. Finally the faint lapping sound came into focus, then some birdcalls. Avery was sure that they were somewhere very isolated, a million miles from civilization.

The men came back into the cabin, and she heard stuff being unloaded; then a match was struck.

"Where am I?" Avery asked, trying to sound vulnerable. She wanted these men to start thinking that she wouldn't do anything rash, that she was a nice sweet girl. Then they would let down their guard and she could make her move.

"You're right smack-dab in the middle of fucking nowhere, doll," the nasal guy said. Then he let out a high-pitched laugh.

"Let me elaborate on that statement: you're on a tiny island on a big lake right smack-dab in the middle of fucking nowhere," her other captor said.

"Where is nowhere?" she asked.

"Nowhere is the Adirondacks, that's where nowhere is."

Avery knew the Adirondack Mountains were about three hundred miles north of Manhattan, and that much of the area was wilderness.

"Could you please take off my blindfold?"

"Oh yeah sure, sweetheart, we're gonna take off your blindfold. And then we're gonna give you our guns, and hail you a helicopter home. Dream fucking on."

"We're just doing our job, kid, nothing personal. But that doesn't mean we won't kill you if we have to. How about a cup of coffee?"

"Sure," Avery said.

Pretty soon the smell of fresh-brewing coffee filled the cabin.

"How you take your coffee?"

"Milk and sugar," Avery said.

"Sorry, doll, we don't have milk."

"And we don't have sugar."

They laughed.

"But we do have guns."

"And we know how to use them."

Avery felt her mouth go dry, her muscles tense. "Never mind the coffee," she said, turning her body to the wall.

"Whatever," the Bronx guy said. They poured their own coffee and went outside.

The hours passed slowly, agonizingly. A faint wash of light seeped through the bottom of the blindfold. The fading light marked the passage of time. The two men talked a little, smoked cigarettes, and listened to bad music on a scratchy radio.

Lying there on that itchy blanket, Avery had a lot of time to think about the tiny life growing inside her. It was part of her. Dependent on her in a way that nothing in her life had ever been before. She felt an overpowering, exhilarating sense of connection and responsibility, devotion and love. It swept through her body and made her skin tingle. And then she knew, with a certainty that echoed in her bones: *she was going to have the baby.* And raise it. And love it as much as any child had ever been loved. It didn't matter that Marcus was the father. *She* was the mother. Avery forgot about her aching muscles and her lingering headache. There was only one thing that mattered. She made a silent vow to her baby: *I'm going to get you out of here alive.*

When darkness descended, the men turned on a light in the cabin.

"How about a bologna sandwich?" one of them asked her.

"No, thanks," Avery answered.

"Suit yourself, sweetheart."

The men ate outside. Then one of them came back in. A little while later she heard his nasal snoring.

Then from the radio, faint and full of static: "We take you now to the headquarters of Flair Cosmetics, where co-owner Parker Adams is having a news conference about the kidnapping this morning of company founder Avery Wilkins. A visibly shaken Ms. Adams is about to read a statement."

There was the sound of commotion, shutters clicking and cameras whirring. Then Parker came on: "I just want to assure you all that every effort is being made to find Avery, and to bring whoever is responsible for this terrible crime to justice," she said, fighting to retain her composure. "I'd like to say something to her kidnappers: Please please *please* don't hurt my friend. Just let her go. I'll give you as much money as you want, just let her go free."

"Parker, will you go ahead with the Charm launch?" a reporter shouted.

"That was a difficult decision to make, but yes, we are going to go through with the party. It's what Avery would want, I'm sure of it. This company is her life, and I'm not going to let it falter. That's all I have to say, thank you all."

That narcissistic psychopath. She wanted Avery out of the picture so that she could have the spotlight all to herself at the Charm party—*and* the kidnapping allowed her to play the part of the distraught friend. Avery seethed. She clenched her teeth, felt her headache coming back. Then she moved her bound hands down to her stomach and rested them there. Within seconds she felt her breathing calm down and her muscles relax.

She had her baby.

And she had a plan.

The Bronx guy came back into the cabin and walked over to Avery. She could smell whiskey on him. He ran his hand down her shoulder. Avery shuddered. "How you doin', doll?"

"Please don't touch me."

"I'll do whatever the fuck I want to you. You're just lucky I got morals."

"It's a little chilly. Do you think I could get a blanket?"

"Sure thing, doll."

A few moments later he draped another coarse wool blanket over her.

Avery turned toward the wall. She stilled her body and slowed her breathing—in and out, in and out. She wanted the thugs to think she had fallen asleep. At the same time she gently wriggled her wrists back and forth, slowly loosening the rope, millimeter by millimeter.

She kept this up as the night hours slowly passed. Then, finally, she heard the second kidnapper begin to snore.

At last the rope loosened just enough for Avery to slip one wrist free. It was an exhilarating moment but she made sure to keep up her rhythmic breathing—in and out, in and out. She curled into a fetal position and silently brought her free hand up to the blind-fold. She pushed it up just enough so that she could peek out.

Slowly, silently Avery turned her head and looked around the bare-bones cabin. The nasal guy, asleep on the cabin's other bed, was a huge, hairy hulk. The Bronx guy was short and wiry. He was sleeping in a chair, his chin buried in his neck. There was a metal lamp on the bedside table next to her. A coffeepot on the small stove. A gun on the table.

Avery turned her head back toward the wall. She put her hand on her stomach. *I'm going to get you out of here alive.* She reached down and began to loosen the ropes that bound her ankles.

There was a splash out on the lake.

"*What!*" The thug in the chair started awake.

Avery froze.

The nasal guy bolted up in bed. "What's wrong?!"

"You hear something?"

"No."

"You sure?"

"Yeah, I'm sure. It's quiet."

"Too quiet."

"What's happening?" Avery asked in a groggy voice. At the same time, she slid her free wrist back into the rope.

"I don't know, what *is* happening?" the Bronx guy said suspiciously.

He crossed to her bed and stood over her. Then he yanked up the blanket and checked her out.

"Brrrrrrr, I'm cold," Avery said.

"Well, excuse fucking me," he said, before dropping the blanket.

"Thank you."

"Hey, maybe I was just dreaming," the Bronx guy said. "But I think it's my turn to get the bed."

"All right, all right," the nasal guy said.

They traded places and within a couple of minutes the thug on the bed was sound asleep.

Avery heard a cap being unscrewed. Then the smell of whiskey and the sound of it being poured into a mug. Good, he was drinking. It would dull his reflexes.

"Aaah . . . ," the man sighed, smacking his lips. A match was struck, and soon dense cigar smoke mingled with the whiskey fumes.

She waited and listened and breathed—in and out, in and out.

More whiskey was poured. The cigar went out.

And then finally she heard him snoring, a loud drunken snore.

They were both asleep.

Under the blanket, Avery slipped her hand out of the rope. She reached down and worked the rope around her ankles. It loosened a little, and then a little more. Still breathing—in and out, in and out—she worked the rope until she could slip free.

It was time.

59

AVERY PUSHED OFF the blindfold. She turned away from the wall, and in one silent stealthy move lifted the blanket and slipped her feet to the floor.

The floorboard creaked.

The goon asleep in the chair opened his boozy eyes.

Avery grabbed the bedside lamp and smashed it over his head—hard.

He moaned and then slumped over, out cold.

The guy in the bed bolted up but Avery was out the door.

It was dark, but in the moonlight she could make out the shape of a canoe. She ran to it and desperately pulled it over the ground toward the water. Then she was grabbed from behind. She reached into the canoe and grabbed the oar. She swung around with all her might and smashed it into the man's head. He screamed and let go of her.

Avery got the canoe into the water and hopped into it. She began frantically to paddle away from the island, out into the black water.

She heard the men yelling at each other. Then a flashlight swept its beam across the lake.

A shot rang out—*ping!*—and exploded in the water a foot from the canoe. There was a tiny island up ahead, not more than a rock outcropping. She rowed with a strength she didn't know she had, pulling the canoe through the freezing black water, stroke, stroke, stroke. She reached the island and maneuvered the canoe behind it as more shots rang out.

Avery held on to a scrubby branch and steadied the canoe. Her heart was pounding in her chest so loudly she thought it might burst. She gulped air. The thugs' bitter curses rang out over the lake. As Avery's eyes adjusted to the moonlight, she could make out the shore. There was a small dock and a dirt road leading away from it, through the woods.

A shot rang out and hit the rock. Then another. Avery slipped out of the canoe and into the water. It was cold but she didn't feel it. She dove down and swam with every ounce of her strength and will—*I'm going to get you out of here alive*—pulling herself through the cold black water—*stroke-stroke-stroke* until her lungs were about to burst. She broke the surface and gulped oxygen. The flashlight was sweeping the water. A shot rang out. But there, up ahead, was the dark outline of the dock.

She swam silently, stealthily toward it.

60

AVERY REACHED THE dock and swam to the far side. In the safety of the shadows, she made her way to shore, crawled out of the water, and made a dash for the dirt road. Behind her she heard more shots and echoing curses.

The road turned out to be little more than a narrow, overgrown track. She started down it, shivering and barefoot. Within seconds insects were swarming around her head and branches were scratching her skin. But she had to keep moving. She broke off a branch and used it as a swatter. She looked up at the night sky. Judging from the position of the moon, it was well past midnight. Daybreak was hours away. She found the North Star and then the Big and Little Dippers. She was heading east.

Avery put one foot in front of the other and just kept moving. Every twenty minutes or so she would stop and stand still, listening for any possible sounds of civilization. But all she heard were the sounds of the woods: animals scurrying, cawing, slithering, and stalking. And then there was the sound of her own heart, beating like an angry drum.

As the hours passed, her throat grew parched and she felt light-headed from hunger. Her body was covered with bites and scrapes, but she just kept walking, her mind and heart focused on one thing: *I'm going to get you out of here alive.*

The road and the night seemed endless and Avery began to flush, then shiver, then sweat. A fever took hold of her, and soon there was nothing but the next step, just take the next step, push through the branches, swat the bugs, just take that next step.

Finally a dim gray glow lit the horizon. Avery's body was heavy and hot but she pushed on.

Then her legs went out from under her and she crumpled to the ground.

I'm going to get you out of here alive.

Avery pulled herself to her feet.

Then she heard something. She stilled herself and listened. It was faint, but unmistakable: *whoosh . . . whoosh . . . whoosh . . .*

Tires on a road.

A fresh jolt of adrenaline swept through her, and she moved faster, pushing the branches away, ignoring the pain, the fever, the hunger. The sky grew brighter, the sounds of tires closer. And then there it was, up an embankment: a road. Avery staggered up the slope, closer, closer . . .

Then she blacked out.

61

AVERY FELT SOMETHING damp and warm on her face, pulling her back into consciousness.

"There you are, dear, there you are."

An older woman was looking down at her, a warm smile on her deeply lined face, as she gently ran a washcloth over Avery's forehead. She was in the world's softest bed and her body felt heavy, but soothed. She put a hand on her stomach. *They were safe.*

"When I saw you lying there by the side of the road, I almost had a heart attack. I thought you were dead at first," the woman said. "I was going to take you to the hospital, but it's so damn far and once you began stirring, I could tell you weren't hurt too bad. Hell, I looked worse after my snowmobile accident. So I brought you here and cleaned you up, put some antiseptic on your cuts and bites."

Avery managed a grateful smile. The bedroom was snug, with knotty-pine paneling and floral plates on the wall.

"I can't imagine what happened to you," the woman said.

"What time is it?"

"It's ten-thirty. You've been asleep for hours."

"I have to use your telephone."

"Don't you think you should rest a bit more?"

"I have to use the phone."

Avery swung her legs over the side of the bed. Pain shot through her body, but she stood up. She had on a flannel nightgown, about three sizes too large.

"It's out there," the woman said.

The small living room was jammed with overstuffed furniture. Through the front window Avery could see that the small house sat in the woods, down a long driveway.

"I'm Louise," the woman said. "This is my place."

"I'm Avery and I owe you the world's biggest thank-you."

"We're all in this together now, aren't we?" Louise said. She sat at a round table, lit a menthol cigarette, and took a sip from a mug that read "Who Needs God When You've Got Coffee."

"By the way, where am I?" Avery asked.

"Outside Tupper Lake."

Avery sat on the couch and dialed.

Justin's "Hello" was anxious.

"It's me," Avery said.

"Oh, *thank God*—are you all right?"

"I seem to be."

"I have been a wreck, a mess." He sighed deeply and Avery could hear the tension pouring out of him. "Okay, what happened, where are you? Tell me *everything*."

Avery told him the story of her kidnapping, escape, trek through the woods, and rescue.

"That woman is a saint."

"St. Salem."

"I've been up all night and went through two packs myself, but I suddenly feel full of piss and vinegar. First, I'm going to call the state police. Then I'm going to notify the media. Parker has insisted on going ahead with the party, but I think we should cancel."

"No way. I want the party to go on as planned."

There was a short pause. "Okay, kiddo, you got it. I'll charter a plane to Lake Placid and should be at the cabin in a matter of hours. That'll give you enough time to talk to the police. Then we'll head back to the airport. Put the saint on so I can get her info. See you soon—you did good."

Louise made Avery a country breakfast of eggs, bacon, and pancakes. Food never tasted so good. Then she soaked in a hot bath until the state police arrived.

There were two officers, one young and one near retirement. They knew who Avery was from the coverage of her kidnapping. She recounted her ordeal, including her conviction that Parker was behind it all. They spread a map out on Louise's table. Louise pointed out the spot on the highway where she had discovered Avery. From there it was easy to trace Avery's route down an old logging road to the lake.

"That's Bluebird Lake," the older officer said. "It's owned by the Clarkson family, has been for over a hundred years. They're a rich family out of Philadelphia."

"Parker's mother is a Clarkson from Philadelphia," Avery said.

The young office got on his phone. Headquarters ordered a state police helicopter dispatched to the lake. The officers were told to stay with Avery. Louise made a big pot of coffee and thawed some cinnamon buns. A half hour later the troopers got a call: the two kidnappers were in custody and had already confessed that they were working for Parker Adams.

"Well, this case is going to be wrapped up pretty darn quickly," the older trooper said.

Avery excused herself and went into the bathroom. She leaned in close to the mirror and looked into her eyes. She realized that what she was seeing for the first time had been there all along; it was just that she had never been able to recognize it before: she was capable of anything. She had nothing more to fear.

Not even motherhood.

Whatever she'd faced growing up, the sad dark days, the anguish and abuse, whatever disappointments she'd had in life, in business, in love, even the loss of Finn—all of it had made her stronger. It was as if the door of the little prison of doubt she sometimes found herself in had been flung open and sunlight was flooding in.

As she turned off the bathroom light and went out to wait for Justin, she knew that she was, that she always would be, free—free of her fears, free of her demons, free to be everything she could be.

62

IT WAS THE next day and Avery and Justin were in her office watching a replay of Parker's arrest. The footage on CNN showed her being led out of her downtown loft in handcuffs and put into a police car. Behind enormous sunglasses her face was defiant. Her bail was set at five hundred thousand dollars, and it was expected that it would be met within hours and she would be free pending trial. Still, the damage was done. Avery's lawyers had assured her that she would have no problem winning control of the company from Parker.

Avery clicked off the television and said, "I'm trying not to gloat."

"You're not doing a very good job."

"Parker got what she deserved. She wouldn't have been sorry to see me dead."

"Well, you're very much alive. And since you're here in the office, I think we should at least make a pretense of doing some work," Justin said. "Unless you'd rather talk about what you're going to wear to the party tomorrow night."

"A little dress by Marc Jacobs. Black and white, clingy and hot. And not *too* expensive."

"You can afford it. The factory can barely keep up with all the orders for Charm. Every store in the country wants to carry it, and online sales are through the roof."

"You know what the most amazing part of all this success is?"

"What?"

"I'm actually letting myself enjoy it."

"You're definitely glowing."

"There's another reason for that. I'm going to have the baby, Justin."

"Oh, Avery, that is *wonderful* news."

"I'm meeting Brad this evening."

"So he's the father?"

"No, he isn't. That's what I have to tell him."

63

AVERY AND BRAD were walking through Central Park. It was twilight and the park was bathed in soft radiant light. They reached the Model Boat Pond, the site of their first kiss. A couple of children were still sailing their tiny craft from shore. They sat on a bench, side by side, not touching. Avery felt a cautious anticipation between them, as if they were on the edge of a precipice, about to take a leap of faith.

"Have you forgiven me for not telling you about my wife's death?" Brad asked finally.

"Let's just say I've accepted it," Avery said. "From what I've read I know you behaved honorably."

"I tried my best. The whole experience was very sad. But it forced me to grow up."

"It's funny how that happens," Avery said. "It would be unfair of me to be too harsh on you, since you're not the only one who's been withholding information."

Brad looked at her.

"I don't come from a nice middle-class family. I didn't have an apple-pie childhood."

Avery told him the truth about life at 9 Mayflower Street. As she spoke, the hurt was still fresh, but the shame was gone. In fact, Avery felt a sense of pride. It wasn't a childhood she would have wished on anyone, but it was *her* childhood. Part of the woman she had become.

"And next month I'm moving my mother to a wonderful home out in Queens," Avery said in finishing.

Brad took Avery's hand and said simply, "I can't wait to meet her."

It was exactly the right thing to say. They sat in silence for a few moments.

"I'm glad you're in an accepting mood," Avery said, "because there's something else I have to tell you."

"All right."

"I'm just going to come right out and say it. I'm pregnant. And Marcus is the father."

Brad blinked and clenched his jaw. He ran his fingers through his hair and sat forward, elbows on knees. Finally he looked at her and said, "Before I say anything, I'd like to know how *you* feel."

"I want to have this baby. . . . But my romantic relationship with Marcus is over. Of course he'll remain in my life as the father of my child."

"I understand that."

Avery looked into Brad's eyes. "I want to be with you, Brad. And I'm afraid now that I'm pregnant with another man's child, you won't want me."

Brad leaned back on the bench and exhaled with a deep sigh. Then he took Avery's hand and interlaced their fingers. "I knew I wasn't the only man in your life. This doesn't change my feelings. I want us to be together."

He cupped her face in his palm. Avery's eyes welled with tears.

"I wish you were the father," she whispered.

"We'll just have to have one of our own," he said.

As the lights of the city came on around them, they kissed.

64

THE YACHT WAS festooned with lights, floating in the shimmering, inky waters of the East River like a sparkly dream.

Avery, Brad, and Justin were together in the limousine. It pulled up and they took a moment to savor the sight.

"Well, kiddo, I think you have officially arrived," Justin said.

"*We've* arrived," Avery said.

The driver opened the door for them and Avery stepped out into a blaze of flashbulbs. She slipped her arm through Brad's. He escorted her down the red carpet toward the gangplank.

They passed a pretty young celebrity journalist who gently steered Avery in front of her camera.

"I'm here with the woman of the hour," she said to the camera, "Avery Wilkins, the founder of Flair Cosmetics and the creator of Charm. How are you feeling?"

"Charmed," Avery said.

"Is there anything you want to say to our viewers?"

"This night is the fulfillment of my dreams. Getting here wasn't always easy." Avery looked right into the camera. "I believe every woman can make her dreams come true. It takes sweat and courage and faith."

When they finally stepped on board the yacht, people rushed at Avery from all sides: celebrities, socialites, CEOs. She was glad Brad was there for protection. They moved through the crowd, accepting congratulations, greeting employees. Avery saw Lucy and waved her over.

"Brad Henry, this is my sister, Lucy Charles."

"Wow, sis, you weren't kidding, he's a dreamboat," Lucy gushed. "Do you have a brother for me? A cousin maybe? Heck, I'll settle for a casual acquaintance."

They all laughed

"Listen, can I leave you two for a moment?" Avery said.

Avery slipped away, away from everyone, and found a far corner of the deck, quiet and deserted. She looked out at the swirling currents of the East River and up to the blazing lights of the city. She thought of Finn. There would always be a part of her heart that belonged only to him. The love he gave her lived on and guided her. Avery put her hands on her stomach and felt the life growing inside her. She was ready to be a mother, to love and guide a child.

Avery Wilkins had finally proved herself to the most important person: Avery Wilkins. She looked up at the night sky. Above her was the towering, glittering expanse of the Brooklyn Bridge—leading to a bright tomorrow.

Get what you want!

A new fragrance with a story behind it.

Charm!
All My Children

Available March 2008 at